FIVE SHOTS LEFT

When you have only five shots left, you have to make each one count. Like the outlaw whose quest for revenge didn't go quite according to plan. Or the cowboy who ended up using a most unusual weapon to defeat his enemy. Then there was the storekeeper who had to face his worst fear. A down-at-heel sheepherder who was obliged to set past hatreds aside when renegade Comanches went on the warpath. And an elderly couple who struggled to keep the secret that threatened to tear them apart . . .

BEN BRIDGES

FIVE SHOTS LEFT

Complete and Unabridged

LINFORD
Leicester

First published in Great Britain in 2015

First Linford Edition
published 2016

Lonigan Must Die! first appeared in *A Fistful of Legends* (Express Westerns, 2009)
Copyright © 2009 by Ben Bridges
Comanche Reckoning first appeared online at *www.benbridges.co.uk* © 2006 by Ben Bridges
Stretch-Hemp Station first appeared in *Where Legends Ride* (Express Westerns, 2007)
Copyright © 2007 by Ben Bridges
The Medicine of Takes Many Horses and *The Hanging Gun* are all original to this collection.

A catalogue record for this book is available from the British Library.

ISBN 978–1–4448–2679–1

Published by
F. A. Thorpe (Publishing)
Anstey, Leicestershire

Set by Words & Graphics Ltd.
Anstey, Leicestershire
Printed and bound in Great Britain by
T. J. International Ltd., Padstow, Cornwall

This book is printed on acid-free paper

This is for Richard 'Froggy' Palmer

~

'Ello, boi, 'ow ahh ya?'

Contents

Lonigan Must Die!

Given that he'd once been called the most dangerous man in the territory, Jesse Rayne proved to be a model prisoner. He kept to himself, said *yes sir* and *no sir* and never, *ever* made trouble — which was odd, because Rayne had spent practically his entire *life* making trouble.

Thus, his willingness to toe the line in prison raised more than a few eyebrows . . . until the authorities decided the injuries he'd sustained prior to his last arrest had finally taught him the error of his ways: that the near-constant pain of two broken ankles that never healed properly was a harsh lesson, and one he'd taken to heart.

Still, there was a method to Rayne's madness.

Even before he was delivered to the Pen he'd started planning his escape.

But when he finally saw first-hand how things were, he'd had to think again. For what chance did a man have of escape when he spent most of his days chained to the floor of a dark, cramped cell that was oven-hot by day and colder than a pie-safe by night? And even supposing he *could* escape, if by some miracle he could breach white-washed walls three feet thick, just how far could he get on two ruined legs?

So he came at it from a different direction, settled on just minding his manners and doing as he was told. He took everything they threw at him and the warden and his men slapped themselves on the back and told each other that the system worked after all: that they'd broken him, and he was no longer a threat to society.

How wrong they were.

In one respect, however, they were right on the money. They *had* broken him. For he no longer craved the pulse-hammering thrill of a stage or train hold-up. The pleasure he'd once taken from seeing fear in his victims' eyes, the thrill of the chase, the dry rustle of stolen ten- or twenty-dollar bills between his calloused fingers . . . these things, once so vital to him, were now as nothing. Now only one prospect offered that same heady thrill.

And so he thought about it hour after hour, day after day, night after night, and that was how he got through eight long years of prison life.

Lonigan must die.

*   *   *

The judge had sentenced him to twenty-five years. Given Rayne's track record, he said he'd have normally recommended hanging, but figured Rayne had already suffered enough, what with his ankles and all.

Rayne only shrugged when the sentence was passed. Arrogant as ever, the prospect of a quarter-century behind bars didn't scare him. There were ways and means to shorten a prison term,

5

and eventually he employed them all. He attended church services regularly and spent hours whittling exquisitely detailed figurines for the authorities to sell at their public bazaars each Sunday, and with the help of the prison librarian he even learned to read and write.

Then the day he'd worked so hard for finally arrived.

He was called before the warden, who informed him that he was satisfied from the conversations he'd had with his staff that Rayne was a changed man. The warden used the word *reformed*, but what he really meant was *crushed*.

'But tell me, Jesse,' he went on, 'what have you learned from your time here?'

Rayne wanted to say, *Never get caught*. Instead, he said in a low, bubbly exhalation, 'There's always a consequence to a man's actions, Warden. He makes a bad move, it's usually a bad consequence.'

Rayne could tell by the smile that spread across the warden's ruddy face that the answer pleased him.

The warden said, 'You understand, of

course, that I can make no promises?'

'Yes, sir.'

'However, I truly believe in my heart that you have become a new and better man during your internment, and I would like to see you live out the remainder of your days in peace and freedom, and give something positive back to the society you terrorized for so long. That will be my recommendation to the parole board.'

★ ★ ★

The warden was as good as his word. The parole board met and discussed the case the following week, after which Rayne was summoned again.

'We are of the opinion that you have paid your debt to society and learned important lessons about civilized conduct. It is therefore the recommendation of this board that you walk free . . . on parole, of course.'

Rayne strained to keep his expression neutral. It would be disastrous to allow anything other than humility and gratitude to show on his lean, prison-pale face now. At last he said, 'I'm beholden, gentlemen.'

And he even managed a tear for them, just to prove it.

$$\star \quad \star \quad \star$$

He left the Pen the following morning, limp-shuffled through the ornate adobe archway they called the sallyport and there beneath the shadow of the guard tower and its big Hotchkiss gun, he drew in the first really *free* air he'd breathed in almost three thousand days.

In town, using some of the money the prison administrators had held for him, he bought a ticket for the first train north. Easing down onto a hard seat, he pulled his black hat low, crossed his arms and tried to sleep. But sleep at this late stage was impossible. After so many years of just minding his manners and following orders, his sluggish blood was finally starting to stir again with the anticipation of what was to come.

And why not? He *owed* Lonigan. Owed him *plenty*.

At the time of their encounter he'd been riding alone with a mad-as-hell posse dogging his back-trail. The robbery of a copper mine payroll at Organ Pipe Creek four weeks earlier had made things uncomfortably hot for him and his gang, and fearful of capture, the men had deserted him in ones and twos during the long chase west.

So he rode alone and on the dodge from a pursuit party that just wouldn't quit. But he was finally closing on the Colorado River. If he could make a safe crossing and lose himself in California, he could rest up for a while, spend his share of the payroll money and then set about putting a new gang together.

Thus, when he came down out of the Buckskins that cool September evening and rode into Apache Wells, it was simply to stock up on supplies before making one last push for the border.

The town was little more than two parallel streets between facing rows of false-fronted business premises, the streets surrounded by a haphazard scattering of timbered houses and spindly shade trees.

It was a little after six and the sun was already starting to set. First Street was quiet, this being the supper hour, and the owner of Dean's Mercantile was just fixing to close up for the night when Rayne dismounted out front and threw a loop at the hitch-rail. A saloon sat almost directly across the street, and he was tempted to go grab a drink, but decided to get his provisions first.

He went inside and glanced around. The store smelled of leather, coffee, pickled fish and peppermint balls. Hams, pots and skillets hung from the low rafters.

Hearing the hollow thud of Rayne's boots on the worn floorboards, the storekeeper turned, set his broom aside and nodded tersely. He was tall and thin, with fine red-fair hair and lifeless green eyes behind small, round spectacles. 'Help you?' he asked.

'Need a few things.'

'Sure. What'll it be?'

He asked for plug tobacco and coffee, a handful of cheap cigars, some spruce gum, a selection of canned goods, some bacon and cheese. The storekeeper fetched everything and stacked it neatly on the counter. As an afterthought, Rayne added a couple of work shirts to his order, some new socks, and a bottle of bald face whiskey that the storekeeper filled from the spigot of a barrel in the right-hand corner.

'That it?'

'That's it.'

The storekeeper took a pencil from behind his ear and started to make a total on a scrap of paper beside the cash register. Rayne watched his lips work silently.

If he'd had any sense he would have paid for his supplies and rode on with no-one the wiser that he'd ever passed through. But because it had always been Rayne's way to impose his will on others, he slipped his New Model Army .45 from leather and pointed it at the storekeeper's belly.

'If it's all the same to you,' he said, 'I'll just consider all this as a gift.'

He expected the storekeeper to raise his hands, take a backward pace and stammer something along the lines of, 'S-sure, mister, just . . . just don't hurt me.'

But instead all pretence at civility leeched from the storekeeper's face and suddenly he looked old, worn down — and mad.

'The hell you will,' he replied.

Rayne stiffened as if slapped.

'You know what I make from selling a strip of candy here, a few yards of cloth there?' the storekeeper demanded, speaking fast and low. 'Pennies, mister, *pennies*! So if you think I'm gonna let you take what you want, just 'cause you've got a gun in your hand — '

Rayne slapped him across the face

with the Colt. The sight opened a gash in the storekeeper's right cheek and his legs folded. He clung to the edge of the counter to keep from collapsing altogether.

Holstering his gun, Rayne reached for the provisions, but as he did so the storekeeper grabbed his wrists and clung tight.

'*You'll have to kill me before I let you walk out of here without paying!*' the storekeeper grated.

Rayne's temper flared. He tried to yank his hands free, but the storekeeper's grip was tight and all he did was pull the man forward, over the counter, taking the provisions with him. They crashed to the floor, and the storekeeper, damn him, started yelling.

Rayne had spent weeks dodging the law and was now so close to the border that he could almost taste freedom. He didn't need any more trouble at this late stage.

Deciding to cut his losses, he turned and started for the door, but the storekeeper, still sprawled on the floor and screaming at the top of his lungs, grabbed him around his left calf in an attempt to keep him from getting away. Rayne staggered, caught his balance, turned and stamped on the store-keeper's face, but that only made the storekeeper scream louder and hang on tighter.

Again Rayne tried to drag his leg free.

Bleeding from the nose now, blood-smeared teeth bared in a determined grimace, the storekeeper clung on, yelling, '*Help! I'm being robbed!*'

Rayne drew his .45 again, thumbed back the hammer and shot him square in the face. Within the confines of the store, the gun-blast was deafening. The storekeeper's head disappeared in a red spray. His arms and legs twitched.

Pulling himself free at last, Rayne ran through the doorway, out into the lantern-lit evening — and straight into the man he eventually came to know as Lonigan.

★ ★ ★

The collision took both men by surprise. Rayne lost his grip on his Colt and dropped it with a thud to the boardwalk. Instinctively he bent to retrieve it, but Lonigan brought up a knee that slammed him backwards.

For the second time that evening Rayne saw red. He came up against one of the store's double doors and got his first real look at his opponent, a tall, slim man about his own age with dark eyes and short, oiled black hair. The rest was just an impression: a creased black suit, a white shirt open at the throat, a grey vest; a townsman, unarmed.

Then Rayne threw himself forward, big fists rising and falling like billy clubs.

Lonigan wilted beneath the onslaught, and Rayne finally put him down with a heavy, downward swing that had his every ounce of muscle behind it. As Lonigan crumpled, Rayne wheeled around and lurched toward his skittish horse. He tore the reins free, grabbed the saddle horn —

Lonigan slammed his palms down on Rayne's shoulders, dug into the folds of his box coat and wrenched him backwards.

Both men spilled to the hardpan, the horse reared up, flailed at the air a few times, then turned and ran.

Rayne elbowed Lonigan in the belly, heard him wheeze, then dragged himself free, pushed to his feet, turned and kicked him in the ribs, once, then again. Lonigan hunched up, his face, clean-shaven, with long dark sideburns, screwed tight with pain.

Around them, the town was coming to life. Rayne heard shouting and turned. Men were silhouetted in the doorway of a saloon on the other side of the ill-lit street, and all at once he grew acutely aware that he was unarmed and afoot. Much as he wanted to keep kicking Lonigan, he knew he had to flee.

For one brief moment he debated stopping long enough to retrieve his

gun, but that might cost him everything. Instead, he resolved to run, find
someplace to hide, then come back
later and steal a horse.

He leapt up onto the boardwalk and
ran, reached a corner and took it. A
pounding similar to that of the blood
thumping in his ears made him chance
a quick backward glance. A silhouette
blurred into the shadow-filled alley behind
him.

Lonigan.

Sweating hard, Rayne ran on. A
yapping dog leapt out of nowhere,
started nipping at his heels, and he
wondered how everything could have
gone so wrong so quickly.

Then he saw the far end of the alley
fill with townsfolk and knew there'd be
no escape that way.

With a curse he turned back to face
Lonigan, and as he did so he realized
that an outdoor staircase ran slantwise
up the side of the store. If he could get
into the premises above, find a gun, a
knife, a hostage, he might turn his

fortunes around yet . . .

He lurched toward the staircase, took the dried-out wooden steps three at a time.

Lonigan thundered up after him.

Rayne kept going, teeth clamped hard, reached the small landing, grabbed the door handle.

Locked.

No matter. He stepped back and shoulder-barged the door. It refused to yield, but he had an idea that the second blow might do it. He braced himself for another attempt, but —

All at once Lonigan was on the landing with him, fists windmilling, and then the door was forgotten as each tried to pummel the life from the other. Rayne grabbed Lonigan by the face, squeezed tight and tried to push him off. Lonigan shook his head free, hit him in the stomach, said something like, 'Give it up . . .'

Rayne managed to turn around and thrust Lonigan backwards off the landing, but before he could fall, Lonigan snatched at the rickety handrail and held on. He surged back, kicked Rayne in the shin and followed the move with a body check. Rayne stumbled backwards, hit the locked door.

Furious now, he launched a punch that would have taken Lonigan's head off had it connected.

But it didn't.

At the last moment Lonigan dodged to one side, and Rayne's momentum carried him forward, past his opponent, over the railing and into thin air . . .

Rayne turned an ungainly somersault and came down hard, landing flat on his feet with a loud splintering of bone. Pain speared through him and he collapsed onto his face, squirming, mewling, his fingers clawing at the dirt.

A lifetime of pain later big hands turned him roughly onto his back. Someone raised a lantern high. Although his vision was blurred, Rayne spotted a badge on the shirt of a big man with a horseshoe mustache.

A circle of faces stared down at him. He wanted to curse them but didn't have the strength. He heard someone say, 'Look at his feet . . . ' And then another face appeared at the lawman's shoulder, the face of the man who'd brought him down.

'Is he still alive?' Lonigan asked anxiously.

The lawman nodded. 'He's alive, all right, Reverend, though he'll be lucky if he ever walks again.'

Rayne frowned.

Reverend?

He'd been beaten by a *preacher?*

For some reason the revelation brought with it an irrational, overwhelming sense of shame.

'But . . . ' said the lawman.

'What is it, marshal?'

'His face . . . '

'What about it?'

The lawman said, 'Do you know who you've bested here, Reverend Lonigan?'

The priest shook his head.

''Less I'm mistaken, you've just tangled with Jesse Rayne — the most dangerous man in the territory.'

★　★　★

When the train finally hauled into Apache Wells, Rayne climbed awkwardly down to the platform. The journey had been long and hard and he felt stiff and slow. He hobbled out of the depot and surveyed the town. Save for the recent arrival of the railroad, the years had hardly touched the place.

Stomach tight, he shuffled across First Street, afraid someone might recognize him from all those years ago and sound the alarm, but no one gave him a second glance. He stopped a woman in hoop skirt and bonnet, doffed his hat and asked her if Reverend Lonigan was still killing sin in those parts. When she confirmed that he was, and by all accounts doing a pretty fine job of it, he released a relieved sigh.

So far, then, so good.

At the nearby livery he dickered for a stocky Indian pony and a cheap eight-string stock saddle, then led the horse out into the street and swung astride.

Cursing the pain the action brought to his damaged ankles, he walked the animal down to what had once been Dean's Mercantile.

A thin young man lounging on the boardwalk outside watched him come. He had blue eyes, straw-yellow hair and a spill of freckles bridging his nose. He was eighteen, maybe a little younger. He wore a blue band-collar shirt and navy Crocker pants, and a brown leather cartridge belt hitched high around his skinny waist.

The kid quickly looked away from him. For some reason Rayne's presence seemed to agitate him; he shuffled his feet, wiped his palms down his shirt-front and then turned on one run-down heel and wandered away.

Dismissing him from mind, Rayne dismounted and hobbled into the general store. The place was quiet. 'Afternoon,' said the clerk, coming through a curtained doorway in the back wall. 'Help you?'

Knowing that he'd be moving hard for the border once he'd settled with

Lonigan, Rayne ordered provisions for three or four days and asked the clerk to put them all in a gunnysack.

'Will that be all?' asked the clerk when he was finished.

Rayne's head filled with echoes from his past, the previous owner saying, 'That it?' just before all hell broke loose.

He shook his head to be rid of the memory, glanced around, found what he was looking for and peered down through the long arc of pilfer-proof glass at the selection of guns beneath. 'Want to buy one o' these,' he said.

'Sure. Which one takes your fancy?'

'The forty-five,' said Rayne.

The clerk picked up the Colt almost reverently, and cradling it in his palm, handed it over. Rayne closed his right fist around its walnut grips and hefted it. He liked its balance. He flipped open the loading gate, thumbed back the hammer, turned the cylinder, checked the chambers, then closed it back up, held it at arm's length, sighted along the short barrel. 'I'll take it.'

'You need a belt for it? We got — '

'No belt. But I'll need a box of ammunition.'

He paid for his purchases, loaded the gun and stuffed it into his waistband, then left the store and tied the gunnysack around his saddle horn before remounting stiffly. The freckle-faced kid watched him from the mouth of a nearby alley. Again their eyes met briefly. Then the kid turned away from Rayne, still unable to meet his gaze for any length of time.

Rayne's attention shuttled to the saloon across the street. All at once he needed a drink to steady nerves that had never in the past needed steadying.

⋆　⋆　⋆

The church was a moderately sized frame building with white clapboard walls, gray shingles and a three-tiered bell-tower. It stood at the far end of Main, just beyond the town, and was enclosed by a neat picket fence that separated it from the scrubby trail west. Rayne tied his horse to the fence and let himself inside, instinctively sweeping off his hat as he did so.

He paused beside the baptismal font and looked around. The building was empty. A narrow aisle led down between fifteen rows of Bible-strewn pews to an altar and an octagonal pulpit. Upon the altar sat a display of flowers; tamarisk mostly, mixed in with Indian hawthorn and desert willow. Bars of dusty late-afternoon sunshine slanted in through the tall, high windows to puddle like molten gold across the floor.

Turning his hat restlessly before him, Rayne shuffled slowly toward the altar. His footsteps echoed off the plain blue walls. There was a strange, throat-tightening sense of unreality to the moment. After eight long years he'd made it, and the vengeance he'd craved for so long was finally about to be his.

He was almost at the altar when a gentle voice behind him said, 'Can I help you?'

He froze.

That voice. He remembered it so well, and to hear it again now left him light-headed.

He turned.

Lonigan stood in the open doorway, and when he came deeper into the church, Rayne was rocked by his appearance. In his mind, Lonigan hadn't changed a notch. The man he'd come to kill had been tall, lean, dark, about his own age. The man he faced now looked somehow shorter, heavier, grayer. It didn't seem possible that eight years could bring about such a change in a man, and yet —

He stopped then, as he realized what he'd just thought.

That he and Lonigan were about the same age.

Did *he* look that old? Had the years ravaged *him* the way they'd ravaged his target? The thought distracted him momentarily and he squinted at his hazy reflection in one of the church windows. He wondered when he'd last looked at himself, *really* looked at himself, and seen not the man he used to be but the old man he'd become.

'Are you all right?' asked Lonigan.

Rayne's eyes shuttled back to him and he said, 'Don't you remember me, preacher?'

Lonigan's dark eyes, duller and heavier-lidded now, narrowed. 'I'm sorry. Have we met before?'

Without warning, Rayne flung his hat aside and smashed a fist into Lonigan's face, and the preacher crashed against one of the pews, knocking it out of alignment. Bleeding from the mouth, he sank to the floor.

'Does *that* jog your memory?' spat Rayne, towering over him. 'It ought to. Eight years ago you ruined my life!'

The echoes of Rayne's voice died and the church went coffin-quiet. At last Lonigan's gaze sharpened and he said softly, 'Is it *really* you, Rayne?'

'It's me.'

'Did you . . . *escape*?'

'No. They figured I'd served my time.'

'And so you came here . . . ?'

' . . . to settle accounts,' said Rayne.

Lonigan considered that for a moment before releasing a trapped breath. 'Then you've come for the wrong man,' he said.

'Huh?'

'You ruined your *own* life, Rayne.'

'The hell I did!'

Clutching the back of a pew, Lonigan dragged himself to his feet. Rayne immediately took a backward pace and tore the .45 from his waistband.

Lonigan stared down at the gun. 'Is this what you thought about while you were in prison?' he asked. 'Killing me?'

'Uh-huh.'

'Is it *all* you thought about?'

'Pretty much.'

To his surprise, Lonigan snorted. 'You're a liar. You served . . . what was it, eight years? And you wasted each and every one of them just thinking about *me*? About *this*?'

'Don't flatter yourself. I thought about plenty else.'

'Such as . . . ?'

'What I could have had, if you hadn't taken my freedom away from me. A wife, maybe. Younkers. A *son*.'

'And what kind of husband do you suppose you'd have made? What kind of father?'

'A lousy one, most like. But I'll never know for sure, will I? Thanks to *you*.'

Lonigan reached into the pocket of his loose-fitting black jacket. Rayne stiffened, but the preacher only tugged out a handkerchief. He dabbed at his mouth. Some of the blood had dripped from his chin onto his white collar.

He looked at Rayne over the square of cloth, shook his head and said, 'I guess you'll never learn, will you?'

Rayne caught the tinge of bitterness in Lonigan's voice and said, grudgingly, 'Learn what?'

'That life's all about choices. That it always *has* been and it always *will* be. Some people make the right ones. Others, men like yourself, don't. They always go for the easier option.

'Well, you face another choice right now, Rayne. You can go ahead and kill me, and spend the rest of your days in jail or on the run, or you can be *better* than that, stronger, set all your hatred aside and stop making the same mistakes over and over.'

Rayne sneered. 'No good appealin' to my better nature, Lonigan. I ain't got one.'

'All men have one. But sometimes a man needs more strength to resist the beast within than to give it free rein.' Unexpectedly, and with an odd, world-weary snort, he added, 'I should know.'

Uneasy now, Rayne said gruffly, 'Why don't you quit talkin' in riddles?'

'All right,' said Lonigan, and took a breath. 'That night we clashed. Did you ever wonder *why* I came after you the way I did? Why I just wouldn't quit?'

Rayne shook his head warily.

'I'll tell you. It's because I was in a mean mood and I welcomed the chance to take it out on someone.'

'Better watch your mouth, Lonigan.

Your halo's starting to slip.'

'It slipped a long time ago,' Lonigan said softly. 'The first time I took a shot of good Kentucky bourbon.'

He saw the surprise in Rayne's cool gray eyes and nodded. 'Oh yes, I've made mistakes as well. My particular vice was whiskey, and eventually my need grew so bad that I could hardly do without it. And yet I couldn't just go into a saloon like other men. As much as anything else I was a mean drunk, Rayne, *really* mean. So I had to drink alone, in shame, and always in fear that someone would discover my secret and drag my dark side into the light of day.'

'I don't need to hear all this . . . ' Rayne muttered uneasily.

'I think you *do*,' countered Lonigan. 'No man can live that way, not forever. I got to the point where I had to make one of those hard choices I just mentioned. I could drink or I could preach, but I couldn't do both. It was a tough call. It would've been easy to tear this collar off and crawl into a bottle.

But I didn't. I fought it. I *tried* to. God, how I tried . . . '

'And that night . . . ?'

'That night I wanted a drink so bad it felt like I had worms burrowing through my brain. It was such a torment that I could've *screamed*. So I went for a walk, figuring to clear my head and get a grip, or so I told myself. But of course I ended up outside the saloon, as I'd known I would, and I thought, the hell with it. I can live without this town and these people and the word of the Lord. I can live without all that. But I can't live another second without a drink.'

Rayne was transfixed by the preacher's tone and manner. Whatever else he'd been expecting from their encounter, it hadn't been this.

Lonigan bowed his head, swallowed hard. 'I had one hand on the batwings when I heard George Dean start yelling that he was being robbed. Then I heard a gunshot and I ran over, intending to help him. Instead, I ran smack into you.'

Lonigan's mouth was a thin, resentful line. 'I was *hurting*, Rayne, hurting bad for a drink, and if you hadn't come along when you did, I'd have gone right into that saloon and got one. You prevented me from doing that. Because of *you*, I couldn't get that drink, and I was overcome with anger. And every bad thing I felt I took out on you.'

'You sonofabitch,' breathed Rayne, his eyes moving briefly to the pulpit. 'You stand up there an' preach to others, but you're no better'n they are.'

'I'm *human*,' said Lonigan, simply. 'But the point I'm trying to make — the *moral*, if you like — is that afterwards, I realized that I'd faced *another* choice that night — to obey my conscience and go to the aid of my fellow man, or to obey my craving and go get drunk. I figured it happened that way for a reason. I still do.'

'So you quit the booze,' said Rayne, wanting a drink himself right then.

'I quit it. But that doesn't mean I don't still *want* it. I do. Every hour of every day. But whiskey would satisfy me for a while, and then I'd sober up again and hate myself for my weakness, and go get another bottle so I could forget that self-hate. For that reason I fight it, and take some small measure of comfort from winning each day's fight.

'So,' he finished, squaring his shoulders. 'What's it to be, Rayne? Do you shoot me? Or for once in your life do you make the harder choice instead, let go of all that spite and actually *make* something of your life? Which course would give *you* the greater satisfaction?'

Rayne made no immediate reply. He stared down at the floor, thinking.

Then he looked up again, thumbed back the Colt's hammer, *cli-cli-click*, and pointed the gun at Lonigan's paunchy stomach.

Lonigan's mouth twitched briefly in a sour smile. 'I guess I was a fool to think I could destroy your life one day and try to save it the next,' he said quietly. And slowly he lifted a Bible from the nearest pew and held it to his chest.

Hardly able to breathe now, Rayne took up the first pressure on the trigger and told himself this was going to feel so *good* . . . When it came, when that report echoed around the church's high ceiling and Lonigan tumbled backwards, clutching himself, knowing he'd been gut-shot and it was going to take him a long, hard time to die, the pain Rayne had nurtured for eight lost years would finally ease.

Wouldn't it?

His finger continued to tighten on the trigger.

Wouldn't it?

Lonigan's knuckles whitened over the Bible as he braced himself for the hammer-blow of the shot.

But now Rayne recalled what he'd told the warden a lifetime before.

There's always a consequence to a man's actions. He makes a bad move, it's usually a bad consequence.

Wasn't that in so many words what Lonigan was saying, too?

He frowned. Had he unwittingly told

the warden what he'd always secretly known to be true?

Gritting his teeth, he thought stubbornly, *Die, you sonofabitch*.

But his finger refused to pull the trigger, and a long ten seconds later he deflated, let the gun drop loosely to his side. And as he finally admitted to himself that Lonigan was right, he managed softly, 'No, preacher. *I* was the fool.'

★　★　★

It was dark when he left the church.

He'd come to kill a man but instead faced a truth he'd never previously cared to acknowledge. Now he felt washed-out and empty. He gathered his reins, set his teeth against the pain in his ankles and mounted up.

Drawing in a deep draught of fresh, free night air, he walked the pony back into town and drew rein outside what had once been Dean's Mercantile. He wanted to believe that this was where all his problems had started, but he understood now that they'd begun long before that night. He thought about all the choices he'd ever made and knew without doubt that, as Lonigan had said, he *had* ruined his own life.

He was just about to tell himself that things would look better in the morning when he suddenly became aware of the gun he'd bought earlier, digging into his side.

The gun.

It came to him then. A gun set him on the road to ruin. Maybe a gun could also end it for him.

Dry-mouthed, he heeled the horse over to the hitch-rack and dismounted. Fifteen feet away, a dark alley — the same alley in which he'd lost his fight with Lonigan all those years earlier — beckoned. He could vanish into its shadows, stick the gun up under his jaw and use the bullet he'd intended for Lonigan on himself. Just one squeeze of the trigger and no more of a life that wasn't a life at all and never really had been.

Oh Lord, it would be so *easy!*

The decision made, he limped up onto the boardwalk and made for the alley-mouth, pulling the gun as he went, and in that moment all further thought ceased for the simple reason that there was nothing left to think *about.*

But as he shuffled into the alleyway he sensed movement in the shadows ahead and abruptly came back to the here and now. Twenty feet away, a short skinny figure hurriedly stepped back from a lighted window just the other side of the outside staircase.

It was the freckle-faced kid.

Seeing him, the kid turned and started to walk away.

Impulsively, Rayne brought the .45 to full-cock. 'Don't you move a muscle!'

Hearing the sound, the kid froze and raised his hands.

Rayne shambled to the window. Beyond the smudged pane lay some sort of cluttered storeroom. The clerk who'd sold him the gun earlier that afternoon sat at a table in the center of the floor, totaling up the day's take. He had no idea he was being spied upon.

The kid murmured over one shoulder, 'I wasn't doin' nothin'.'

Rayne threw him a thoughtful look. 'You ain't done nothin' *yet*,' he corrected. 'But it appears to me like you was planning to do some serious harm to the owner of that store. I reckon you've been trying to screw up the courage to do it all day.'

'Where'd you get a fool notion like that?'

'It's written all over you, kid.'

He glanced back through the window, at the money piled in coin and paper on the table. Time was he'd have been as tempted as this boy. But now . . .

Again he thought about the life he'd thrown away, the family he'd never had, something the warden had said to him a week before, about giving something *back* to society.

'You ever been in trouble before?' he asked.

'No, sir,' said the kid. 'Honest.'

'Then why start now?'

The kid turned to face him. ''Cause I'm at the end of my rope,' he said bitterly. It fairly spilled out of him then: 'I got no folks, no friends, no work, no money, just the clothes I stand in and my gun, an' that's just about the way it's always been for me.'

'I've seen men make good from less than that.'

'*You?*'

'No, not me. I never had the will or the wisdom. But ... ' Rayne let the hammer down and stuffed the Colt back into his waistband. 'What's your name, boy?'

'H-Hilton Gallagher.'

'Figure on sticking around for a while?'

The kid shrugged. 'I got no place else to go.'

'Hungry?' asked Rayne.

Surprise crossed the boy's face. 'Hungry so's my stomach's through to my backbone.' Cautiously he added, 'Why?'

''Cause I think maybe you and me could stand to talk a while,' said Rayne, as an idea occurred to him, a way to make amends. 'That's if you're not too proud to listen to an old man's words?'

The boy looked at him. His Adam's apple bobbed nervously. 'What do you care what happens to me? You don't know me.'

'No. But I know your type. Thirty years ago I was pretty much where you are now, kid, and I made all the wrong choices. You still got the time to make all the right ones.'

And he thought, *Sides, I'm about as lonely as you are, boy, and right now I reckon I could use a son about as much as you could use a pa.*

'I figure I could stand to listen,' Gallagher said at last.

A weight lifted from Rayne's shoulders. 'Well, let's go get us that meal and somethin' to drink,' he said. 'Oh, and let's get one other thing straight.'

'Sir?'

'You're wrong about having no place

to go, Hilt. From here on in, you're going *up* in the world.' And surprising himself, Rayne actually smiled as he added thickly, 'We *both* are.'

The Medicine of
Takes Many Horses

Levi Boone studied the young man before him with obvious concern. Buck Buchanan was a tall, dark, rail-thin boy of about twenty, with a long neck punctuated by a prominent Adam's apple. He was a hard worker with a cheerful disposition and an ever-ready smile, but he wasn't smiling now. 'Fact, the elderly owner of the Tumbling B had never seen the boy look more serious.

'What's the trouble, Buck?' he asked.

'Got to draw my time, Mr. Boone,' the young man replied regretfully, turning his ragged brown hat in his hands.

'Somethin' happened?'

Buck nodded. ''Member my brother Dick?'

'Be hard to forget *that* hellion,' Boone replied good-naturedly.

'He's dead, Mr. Boone.'

There followed a moment of complete silence. Then, shocked to the core, Boone breathed: '*No!*'

'I jus' got the news this mornin', by wire,' said Buck. 'Got hisself killed by a bunch'a Cheyennes in Nebraska.'

'What the hell happened?'

Buck glanced off toward the window, his hazel eyes still a little glassy from the tears he'd so recently shed. Rolling green hills rose in thick-timbered steps toward the great, snow-covered crags that grazed the blue Wyoming sky beyond.

'Way I understand it,' he said, 'he was on a wood-choppin' detail just outside Fort Robinson, when all of a sudden they were hit by this here bunch of Cheyennes. Dick was . . . well, seems there was this one partic'lar Cheyenne, bigger'n all the rest. They call him Takes Many Horses. It was him split Dick's skull with a war club.'

Boone pushed up out of his chair and limped across the office to a sideboard. There he splashed whiskey into two tumblers, then passed one to the young cowboy.

'I'm right sorry to hear that, Buck,' he said, and meant it. 'But I can't say as I'm surprised that somethin' of the sort's finally happened. There's been trouble out that way for weeks now, ever since Dull Knife an' the rest of his heathens broke out of the agency. Army was holdin' 'em there with hardly enough food, water an' shelter to survive the winter, an' they were doin' it a'purpose, because them Northern Cheyennes wouldn't let the Gov'mint send 'em back to Indian Territory. But that don't make it right.'

Stiffly he raised his glass.

'To Dick,' he said. 'May he rest in peace.'

Buck nodded and threw back the spirit in a single swallow. He choked a little at its fiery aftertaste.

'Well,' said Boone, 'they's no call for you to quit on me, son. If it's time you need to attend the funeral, get Dick's affairs in order — '

47

'Army's already seen to the funeral,' Buck replied. 'But there *is* some business I got to handle. Somethin' means I might not be *able* to come back.'

Boone paused. 'An' what might that be, boy?' he asked cautiously.

'I got to kill me this here Takes Many Horses.'

Once more silence filled the office. Slowly, gratefully, the rancher sat down again. He was in his late sixties now, and a lifetime of range work had left him stove-up and arthritic.

'I've knowed you Buchanan boys a long time,' he said. 'Knowed you both when you weren't more'n knee-high to a cricket. I'm real sorry about Dick, you know that. He was a fine feller. But they's no call to lose you both — an' we'll lose you for sure, Buck, you try seein' such foolishness through.'

Buck set his glass down on the desk. 'I'm sorry to hear that, Mr. Boone, I really am. But it's somethin' I got to do.'

'You're still in shock, boy. You're not thinking straight.'

'Oh, I'm thinkin' straight enough, sir. I *knew* nothin' good would ever come of soldierin' for Dick, but his mind was made up to it. So off he went. And now he's dead. And I aim to fix the sonofabitch who killed him.'

'Leave it to the Army. They're out there right now, roundin' up them broncos.'

'It's somethin' I got to do myself, Mr. Boone.'

'An' if I ask you to reconsider? As a personal favor to me?'

Buck looked at his boss, a man he'd known practically his entire life, and the closest thing to a father he and Dick had had since their own father had died on one of Boone's trail-drives a dozen years earlier. 'I'm sorry, sir. You know I respect you more'n just about any other man alive. But my mind's set.'

Boone's lips quirked briefly. 'You Buchanan boys always were stubborn as flap-eared mules,' he grumbled good-naturedly. 'I still 'member how you always got back on the ponies that throwed you till you could best 'em. But this ain't no fractious cow pony we're talkin' about, Buck. This here is a man that's kilt plenty, by all accounts — red *an*' white.'

A new thought suddenly occurred to him.

'How you figure to find him, anyway? Sonofabitch could be *anywheres* by now.'

'*I'll* find him,' Buck said grimly.

'All right,' said Boone, standing up again and wincing with the effort. 'But let's not have any more talk o' quittin'. That sounds too damn' final. Instead, you jus' take all the time you need. But I'll be expectin' you back here for spring round-up. Best you don't disappoint me.'

He reached across the desk and they shook.

'If there's any way I can make it,' Buck promised, 'I'll be here.'

As the youngster closed the door behind him, Boone thought back to the

Lutheran meetinghouse days of his childhood and absently crossed himself.

'May the good God go with you, boy,' he murmured. 'I got me a notion you'll need Him an' all His angels afore you're through.'

★　★　★

Buck was just tying his bedroll behind his saddle when Preacher angled across the yard toward him.

Preacher wasn't a real preacher, of course, though he looked just as tall and somber as the name suggested. They called him Preacher because he never drank, never smoked and never gambled; because he always carried a Bible with him and attended — sometimes even conducted — Sunday services every chance he got. Though he could be a man of strange ways, however, he was by far the best hand on Levi Boone's payroll, and everyone knew it.

A lean-flanked man with wise gray

eyes and a firm jaw that commanded deference, he finally came to a halt before Buck. When he spoke, his voice was curiously mellow for such a tough-looking, hard-riding cowboy.

'Heard about your troubles, Buck,' he said. 'Thought I'd have a word before you left.'

Buck raised a hand. ''Preciate that, Preach. But afore you go any further, I know how you feel about killin' an' such, but they's nothin' you can say that's like to stop me.'

A faint smile appeared on the older man's face. 'I've no intention of stoppin' you, Buck,' he assured gently. 'A man has to follow his conscience, do what he figures is right. You read about that all the time in the Good Book. Take David an' Jonathan, fr'instance. They were just like brothers, an' when the Philistines killed Jonathan, that David, he smote the Philistines right back. Didn't nobody try to stop *him*.'

He fixed his eyes steadily on Buck. 'But the way I hear it, you ain't goin'' up agin no host of men, Buck, you're goin' up agin just the one — an' I know him.'

Buck's eyes saucered. 'You *know* Takes Many Horses?'

'Well, more exact to say I know *of* him. Feller as mean as that, his reputation has a way o' travelin'.'

'So what do you know, Preach? I can use all the help I can get.'

'He's a Dog Soldier,' said Preacher. 'That's one o' the warriors who handles all the fightin' for the tribe. They're the best of the best, Buck — tough, fearless an' hell on wheels in a battle.

'So this here's a serious fightin' Indian we're talkin' about, boy. He *lives* to fight, an' he knows every trick in the book. Figger he's taken more scalps than you had spots that time you an' Dick got the measles. He's a strong warrior, but more than that, they say he's got strong *medicine*.'

'Aw, that's just bull, Preach.'

But Preacher's expression said otherwise. 'The Injuns can get up to some mighty dark tricks, Buck,' he warned ominously. 'The Good Book calls it 'consultin' with demons'. That's why I want to give you somethin' that could be . . . *useful* to you, considerin' the kind of man you're goin' up against.'

'Don't concern me how much medicine this Injun's got,' Buck said fiercely. 'All I know is, I owe it to Dick to send him to the happy huntin' ground.'

'Well, I'm tellin' you, son, Takes Many Horses is one tough *hombre*. Don't underestimate him. The Cheyennes say he's got a kind of magic that protects him.'

'Whatever he's got, it won't do him much good agin a .44-.40.'

'Don't be so sure. Them Cheyennes, they got spirits they can call on — ornery ones.'

'He's just a man, Preach. An' like any man, he can be killed.'

'As you say,' Preacher allowed, not wanting to argue the point. 'But just in case you're wrong . . . '

He put his hand inside his shirt and took out a small battered Bible. He held it out to Buck. The boy shifted awkwardly at the sight of it.

'Aw . . . I ain't much fer readin', Preach. 'Specially that kind. Some of them names . . . they kinda flummox me.'

'You don't have to read it,' said Preach. 'Just keep it close by. An' remember . . . ' He held the Bible up before the other man's face. 'This ain't just a book, Buck. It's a *sword*.'

Buck had no idea what he meant by that, but he didn't want to show any disrespect, so he took the book, almost grudgingly, and shoved it inside his own shirt.

'Wasn't exactly countin' on usin' a sword, Preach,' he said embarrassedly. 'More like a rifle or a pistol. But I surely do thank you fer thinkin' of me this way.'

He gripped the lean, strong hand Preacher offered, then swung astride his horse.

As he rode off he heard Preacher's

voice intoning, 'The Lord bless thee, an' keep thee; The Lord make His face shine upon thee, an' be gracious unto thee; The Lord lift up His countenance upon thee, an' give thee peace . . . '

★   ★   ★

Buck rode into Fort Robinson five days later.

The compound sprawled across a level plain just north of the White River, and within sight of the Red Cloud Indian Agency, which lay no more than half a mile away.

Tying up outside the log-walled administration block, he introduced himself to the commanding officer's adjutant and was given a small, wrapped package that contained Dick's few meager possessions. Then the adjutant had an enlisted man take him out to the post cemetery, which was situated on what they called the 'old side' of Fort Robinson.

When he saw Dick's grave, his spirits

plunged. The few paltry possessions with which he'd signed up, and a poor patch of dirt six feet long and barely two feet wide, didn't seem like much to show for Dick's eighteen years, and Buck suddenly found himself hoping that he would live longer and amount to more.

'I knew your brother,' said the enlisted man, who was tall and flat-bellied, with fair hair worn spiky-short beneath his kepi. 'He was a good kid.'

Buck turned to him. 'What do you know about the Injun that killed him?'

''Bout as much as I know about any other Injun,' the enlisted man replied with a snort. 'You spend any length o' time out here, they all blur into one after a while. All you know is to kill them before they kill you.'

'Well . . . you got a chief of scouts hereabouts?'

'Sure. Feller name of Lester Spur-beck.'

'He around?'

'You could try the sutler's store.'

'Thanks.'

As it turned out, Spurbeck wasn't at the sutler's store, but Buck eventually found him checking out a string of newly-purchased pack mules in a corral behind the stables.

The chief of scouts was a thin, shifty-eyed man in grease-stiff buckskins, about thirty years of age, with a lank mustache that matched the mousy shade of his long, shaggy hair. After Buck told him what he had in mind, the scout took an old corncob pipe from between his yellow teeth and said suspiciously, 'Let me get this straight. You want me to get a message to Takes Many Horses, tellin' him you're challengin' him to a fight?'

'A fight to the *death*,' Buck replied. 'There's only one of us can walk away from this.'

'Yeah — the Cheyenne, like as not.'

'Well, I do thank you for the vote of confidence.'

'Jus' tellin' it like it is,' said Spurbeck. 'Takes Many Horses is a *warrior*, mister. You look like you never been in a fight your whole life.'

'I haven't.'

'Then what makes you think you got the beatin' of such a fearsome Injun?'

'I don't. But I know I got to try, else I'll get no peace — an' neither will my brother, I reckon. So — can you see to it or not?'

Surrounded by deep-etched weather-wrinkles, the scout's dark eyes suddenly took on a glint of avarice. 'You *do* know, o' course, that he's not about to come right here to the post or anywheres nearby. I'll have to send one of my best men out to find him, parlay with him. Like to be a hard, difficult task.'

'You'll get paid.'

'How much?' Spurbeck said quickly.

Buck dug into his vest pocket. 'Forty dollars,' he said. 'It's about all I got. You can have twenty now, the rest when you get word back from Takes Many Horses.'

'I'd as soon have all forty up front.'

'I'm sure you *would*. But that's the deal. Take it or leave it.'

With a shrug, Spurbeck reached for the money. 'Leave it with me,' he said. 'Like I say, this is a killer Injun you want to mix it up with. Ain't a thing he don't know about slittin' throats and takin' hair.'

'That's *my* problem,' said Buck. 'You just tell him I'm challengin' him to a duel to the death, you tell him why, an' then git him to name a time an' a place where we can meet up, clear of the fort, clear of his own camp. Tell him he can fetch whatever weapons he fancies, but no tricks, he's to come alone. I'll be there by myself, an' I'll be carryin' this here rifle an' my six-shooter, that's all.'

'Game young rooster, ain't you?' Spurbeck conceded grudgingly. 'All right, I'll see to it — but no guarantees. You'll be stickin' around for a while?'

'Just as long as it takes.'

The scout nodded. 'Minute I hear from him, I'll let you know.'

The next three days dragged by. Buck spent most of the time slumped at a corner table in the sutler's store, staring moodily across the parade ground as he nursed one bitter cup of coffee after another.

He tried to be patient about it. He told himself that trying to find one Cheyenne in country like this was akin to finding the needle in the haystack. It all hinged on Lester Spurbeck, and whoever he sent out to make contact with Takes Many Horses.

But just how hard was that man likely to search for a bunch of killer Indians with no more than twenty dollars up front as an incentive? Not even the promise of a further twenty was likely to make him risk his hide any more than he had to, no matter how impoverished he might be.

Still, if Spurbeck's scout *could* find Takes Many Horses, Buck was sure the Cheyenne would accept his challenge.

He could hardly refuse . . . *could* he?

If Takes Many Horses proved impossible to find, or if he chose *not* to respond to the challenge, then Buck had no idea what he was going to do next. He knew he couldn't just ride back to the Tumbling B and forget about his self-imposed quest. He'd never know peace if he didn't settle things once and for all with Dick's killer.

So all he could do was wait, and hope . . . and then wait some more.

Then, mid-morning of the fourth day, Spurbeck slouched into the store, corncob pipe clamped between his yellow teeth, and dropped into the chair opposite him.

'It's done,' he said quietly. 'Says he'll meet you tomorrow noon, south side of Rib Lake.'

Buck scowled. 'Where's Rib Lake?'

''Bout fifteen miles west, thereabouts. I'll give you directions . . . that is, happen you're still set on seein' this thing through?'

'I am.'

Spurbeck shrugged. 'Your funeral,

kid. Jus' watch yourself, that's all. You mix it up with the likes o' Takes Many Horses, you're gettin' yourself into the kind o' fight you ain't never fought before. An' as we both know, you ain't never fought *any* kind o' fight before.'

Not caring to be reminded of that, Buck reached into his vest pocket and passed over the second twenty. 'Thanks for your help.'

Spurbeck quickly made the money disappear. 'Don't thank me, kid,' he said, puffing smoke. 'Truth to tell, I ain't done you no favors. But I reckon you'll find that out for yourself, soon enough.'

★ ★ ★

Buck hardly slept a wink that night, and was glad to set out for Rib Lake just after sunrise the following morning. The fort fell behind him and flat grass plains unfurled ahead, scored through by long, curving swathes of lodgepole and cottonwood, ponderosa, aspen and white bark. The morning slowly warmed up a little and out ahead he saw pale gray escarpments loom tall against the azure sky. From a distance they resembled the pipes of a church organ.

Following Spurbeck's directions, he found a narrow trail through the rocks and a little before noon came out onto a wooded rise overlooking a timber-belted lake whose clear, ripple-free water reflected the sky like a mirror.

It was a sight to take a man's breath away, and he told himself grimly that if he had to die anywhere, this was as pretty a spot as he could have wished for.

Before pushing on, however, he studied his surroundings carefully. As near as he could tell he was alone, but he cautioned himself to take nothing for granted.

Warily he sent his horse down the slope toward the southern shore. There he dismounted, led the animal across to a deadfall and tethered him.

Silence filled the vast bowl of land in which the half-mile-wide lake sat. He strained his ears but heard no sounds at all — and saw no sign of tern or plover, quail, coyote or squirrel.

The absolute stillness had an unnerving effect on him, and he took another nervous glance at his surroundings, then dragged his Winchester from its sheath and jacked in a round with hands that were nowhere near as steady as he'd have liked. Propping the rifle against the deadfall, he then drew his Colt, eased back the hammer, flipped open the loading gate and checked the loads.

At last, satisfied that the gun was unlikely to let him down when it came to a fight, he slipped it back into its holster and wondered what time it was.

And it was in that moment that he realized he was no longer alone.

★   ★   ★

He had no idea what it was that warned him. He just turned fast, and there, standing no more than five feet away, was Takes Many Horses.

It *had* to be him. There could only be one Cheyenne that big. He stood six feet and maybe more — tall indeed for the usually stocky Cheyennes — and he was broad-shouldered and deep of chest, with long, thick-muscled arms.

He wore his greasy black hair long, with a left-side part, and he dressed in a fringed buckskin shirt, breechclout and fringed leggings, the shirt embellished with what looked like elk teeth, hair, beads and quillwork. His moccasins were decorated, too, Buck saw: these with small, colored shells that formed blue or red triangle shapes.

He started to ask himself how such a big man could have come upon him so quietly, but the question died when he looked into Takes Many Horses' face.

He gasped, and instinctively backed away from the Cheyenne.

Takes Many Horses wore the paint of a Dog Soldier. His wide, flat face was smeared dark red from his hairline to about halfway down his hatchet nose. A white line from which dripped four other white lines bisected his face, etching and accentuating the high ridges of his cheekbones. The lower half was its natural color — dark copper.

His mouth was twisted into a sneer, his spite-filled eyes the color of tarnished gold. On his left arm he carried a circular leather shield across which was painted a crude image of what Buck took to be a long-necked turtle. In his right hand he held a war club —

Buck swallowed.

The same club he'd used to kill Dick.

The boy stood transfixed by the weapon. It was a long, stout wooden shaft to the top of which a rock that was just a little smaller than a melon had been attached by means of a bright yellow strip of cloth, this too decorated with a single line of beads.

It was a simple but devastating instrument of death, and could easily —

But then Takes Many Horses roared and launched himself at Buck, the club whirling around his head. The spell broken, Buck fell back again, ducked a roundhouse swing that had every ounce of the Cheyenne's considerable strength behind it.

There was a splash, and Buck realized he'd backed into the shallows of the lake. He fumble-grabbed for his Colt, drew it and brought it up just as Takes Many Horses shoulder-rammed him with the shield. They went down in a tangle, Buck beneath his heavier adversary. In seconds he was under the cold water, Takes Many Horses astride him and holding him down so that his lungs would flood the minute he could no longer hold his breath.

And in the fall he'd lost his grip on the Colt.

He thrashed wildly beneath the Cheyenne but couldn't unseat him. He tried to reach for the Indian's face, to gouge at his eyes, but his shoulders were pinned beneath Takes Many Horses' knees and he couldn't reach high enough.

Then Takes Many Horses rose off

him for just a moment, but only so that he could slam his weight down again with even greater savagery and knock the air from Buck's straining lungs. Buck's lips parted, the air escaped in a string of bubbles and before he could close his mouth again lake water swirled into it.

At once he started choking, and the more he choked the more he felt blind panic surge through him. He twisted like an eel, this way, that way; that way, this way, and somehow he finally unseated Takes Many Horses.

As he lost his balance, the Cheyenne toppled sideways. He crashed into the water and it exploded up around him. Buck rolled the opposite way, lurched up onto his knees, gasping for air. His Colt was gone; all he had left was his Winchester.

He shoved up out of the water, stumbled for the shore. Behind him, Takes Many Horses came up with a scream of defiance and hurled his shield. It spun like a plate, one feather-bedecked edge slamming hard against Buck's nape. Buck went down with pain jarring through his head, but instinctively rolled aside just as the Cheyenne tried to stamp him with both feet.

All at once the Winchester was forgotten in the sudden, fierce boil of Buck's fighting blood. The boy came up, and with no thought for the consequences charged Takes Many Horses. Bent double, he used his head to butt the Cheyenne in the stomach, but it was like trying to butt a stone wall. Takes Many Horses brought his war club down again, and somehow, more by accident than design, Buck caught his wrist and stalled the blow before it could connect.

They struggled like that for long seconds, each man soaked through and turning the dirt underfoot to mud. They glared at each other, Takes Many Horses seeming to take unholy pleasure from the contest. Then Buck brought the inside edge of his left boot down hard along the length of Takes Many Horses' right shin and stamped hard on the red man's foot.

Startled by the move, the Cheyenne howled, and while he was distracted Buck ripped the war club from his grip and flung it out of reach, then punched him right in the center of the face.

Cartilage snapped and Takes Many Horses howled with the shock of it. Buck hit him again, a roundhouse to the jaw this time, and the Cheyenne's head snapped into profile. A hard left punched it back the other way, and then the young cowhand was like a man possessed, hitting, hitting and then hitting some more, his fists like pistons, pummeling the bigger man's ribs, slapping his arms away when he tried to mount a defense, punishing his face until blood made his knuckles slick.

Under such an onslaught, Takes Many Horses had backed into the shallows again. Now one foot seemed to stick in the mud and he fell. White water foamed around him, and it seemed to break whatever spell had captivated Buck. He pulled up sharp, stood with legs spread over his opponent, shoulders heaving as he gasped for air.

'*Get up!*' he screamed. '*Get up and let's finish this!*'

Takes Many Horses looked up at him from beneath a scowl. His face was oily with water, sweat and blood. His nose was skewed to the left of where it had been just a few moments before, his oiled hair was awry, and in his dark eyes there was fury; fury, surprise and . . .

When Buck saw the fear there he felt a wild surge of elation.

The Cheyenne had come here believing the outcome of their contest to be a foregone conclusion, but more by accident than anything else he'd given Takes Many Horses a run for his money . . . and bested him.

The Indian didn't like that, didn't like it that this boy had been able to summon a strength that had been the equal and more of his own.

'*Get up!*' Buck screamed, a little

crazy now. '*Let's finish this!*'

Instead, Takes Many Horses seemed to ignore him, instead looked up toward the sky, and as he did so he began to sway ever so slightly, and his eyes rolled back in his head, and fleetingly Buck thought that he was going to die; that the beating he'd administered had not just injured him, but killed him.

Then Takes Many Horses raised his arms, palms open and spread outward, and as he did so he sent out a series of long, discordant wails. Blinking sweat from his eyes, Buck felt his skin creep. There was something dark and sinister to the sound, and though he wanted to scream at Takes Many Horses to quit it, to get up and let them finish this, something about the ululating wails tightened his throat and made speech impossible.

Takes Many Horses kept singing to the sky, and that's what it was, Buck realized with a jolt, it was a song.

A *death* song?

Did the Cheyenne even *have* a death song?

But the question was banished from his mind as a chill wind blew up out of nowhere, and he realized that the surface of the lake was beginning to crease with line after line of wavelets, each growing steadily bigger as it rushed toward shore.

Now the breeze grew stronger still, became a wind that shoved at him, pushed him backwards, made him slit his eyes and grimace. The sky turned darker, too, as clouds boiled in to blot out the sun. Abruptly the day turned gray and dismal, and something ominous filled the air.

Instinctively he backed away from the Cheyenne, remembering what Preach had told him just before he'd quit the Tumbling B.

He's a strong warrior, but more than that, they say he's got strong medicine . . .

— and —

Injuns can get up to some mighty dark tricks, Buck. The Good Book calls it 'consultin' with demons' . . .

— and —

Them Cheyennes, they got spirits they can call on — ornery ones.

And as he backed up another pace he remembered something Spurbeck had said:

You mix it up with the likes o' Takes Many Horses, you're gettin' yourself into the kind o' fight you ain't never fought before.

Buck's stomach knotted. Was that what this was all about, then? Takes Many Horses was calling on the spirits to *help* him?

The wind blowing more like a gale now, it was all he could do to keep standing. He leaned into it, tried to go forward again and finish Takes Many Horses before he could sing any more of his songs or prayers or whatever in hell they were, but in that moment the Cheyenne suddenly fell silent.

Around them the weather was in turmoil. Low clouds the color of lead left outdoors scuttled and boiled across the sky. The trees surrounding the lake shook and shivered, waving their branches like

75

souls begging for mercy. And the lake itself — there was nothing tranquil about the water now; it was a raging maelstrom, waves crashing onto the shore with ever more force, hurling foam everywhere.

And the noise!

Buck felt that his ears would start bleeding if the thunderous rush of the wind didn't stop soon. He stood there only with effort, the wind blustering around him, buffeting him, threatening to spill him over.

I'm finished, he told himself. *Preach was right.*

Now Takes Many Horses was climbing back to his feet, standing up to his knees in the choppy shallows, head sunk into his neck, body coiled as if ready to spring. Buck saw the flex of his fingers, and twitch of his wintry, expectant smile, and then he came forward, taking great, unstoppable strides, and all Buck could do was stand there, frozen by his own terror, and wait to be killed.

Move, damn you! Move!

But it was no good — he was

paralyzed by the spectacle before him, of a noon that looked more like dusk, of stormheads that came out of nowhere to boil and writhe like cannon fire, of a gale that tore at him and threatened to tear his breath away —

Reckon I should've paid more mind to you, Preach, he thought.

But it was too late now.

Too late . . .

Then he remembered something else Preach had told him that day:

That's why I want to give you somethin' that could be . . . useful to you, considerin' the kind of man you're goin' up against. This ain't just a book, Buck. It's a sword.

Slitted eyes streaming, head pounding with the rush of the wind, he fumbled in his shirt, tore the buttons open in his haste to reach the small, now sodden Bible he'd stashed there. His fingers closed on it, he tore it free and held it high before him —

'No!'

And as he yelled the word, a flare of

lightning suddenly sizzled across the sky, a fork of it discharging into the very center of the lake. And in the sky, where it had speared itself to the earth, there appeared a ragged tear in the clouds, beyond which Buck saw blue sky again.

The following crash of thunder halted Takes Many Horses in his tracks. He twisted around, looked up — and felt it.

The wind easing.

The clouds parting.

The lake calming.

He turned back to Buck, and in his eyes there was puzzlement laced with disbelief as he looked at the ragged, falling-to-bits Bible Buck held high. He clearly had no idea what it was, only that it carried within it some kind of power.

And in that moment he understood, suddenly, that he could now measure his life in seconds.

Without warning he dodged sideways and sprinted for his war club. Buck watched him go; then self-preservation kicked in and he started running, too

— towards his horse, and his Winchester.

Takes Many Horses bent, scooped up his war club. He turned, screamed his defiance and came charging at the young white man.

Buck dropped the Bible and grabbed up his Winchester, almost dropped it in his haste, then came around and down to one knee, snap-aimed and fired, levered, fired again.

His shots took Takes Many Horses in the center of the chest. Blood punched out of him in two misty sprays as the lead picked him up and threw him back the way he'd come. The club went flying, the Cheyenne himself slammed onto his back and slid a little way through the mud until he came to rest half in, half out of the lake.

As Buck watched, his heels drummed a brief tattoo against the earth, then went still.

He watched the Cheyenne for a long time. He saw no rise and fall of the giant's ruined chest. He approached the corpse warily, looked down into the man's sightless eyes as they stared, unseeing, into a sky that was once more the cleanest and most perfect blue.

And he knew that it was over.

★　★　★

When he finally returned to the Tumbling B a week later, he said very little about what had occurred in Nebraska. The men knew better than to ask him — it was easy enough to guess . . . or so they thought. One thing they knew for sure was that Buck would never have come back until his brother's killer was dead.

On that first evening back, he was unable to sleep. He rolled out of his bunk, slipped on his boots and went outside into the sharp, star-speckled night. For a time he just stood there, admiring the heavens and thinking. He'd done a lot of thinking in the past week.

A little while later, a tall, somber-looking figure appeared beside him.

Before Preacher could open his mouth, Buck said softly, 'Someday I'll tell you the whole of it.'

That was good enough for Preacher. With a nod he turned to go back inside. As he did so, Buck asked, 'Hey, Preach. You goin' to meetin' come next Sunday?'

Preacher stopped and looked back. 'Sure am.'

'Figger I might come along,' said Buck.

Preacher looked into what he could see of Buck's face through the darkness. Then he said, 'Fine. That's fine.'

Just before he went to sleep, Preach touched the bedraggled little book Buck had handed back to him upon his return.

The book that had turned out to be a sword.

And he smiled.

The Hanging Gun

It was a cold, stormy Saturday in late November, and the store had been as quiet as a tomb all day.

To pass the time, Tom Reese decided to inventory his dry goods section, and had been working for about twenty minutes when someone entered the store behind him and said softly, 'Hello, Trigger.'

It had been years since anyone had called him that.

Slowly he turned to face the speaker.

A man of average height and build stood just inside the entrance to the store, feet spread wide for balance, thumbs hooked loosely behind his belt. He was about twenty years old, and he wore an unbuttoned box jacket over a plain, burgundy-colored shirt, the shirt tucked into travel-worn Levis. Buckled at his narrow waist was a well-maintained brown-leather gun belt. The belt's holster was tied low to his left hip, the .45 inside it worn butt-forward.

He was a cross-draw man, then, Tom noted.

The boy's eyes were direct and blue, his nose long, his clean-shaven jaw just a little too heavy. Beneath his tall-crowned gray Stetson his hair was blond and naturally curly. He wore it to just below his nape.

But it was his eyes that Tom came back to. If you knew what to look for, a man's eyes could tell you all kinds of things about him, whether he wanted them known or not. The newcomer's eyes were no different.

This feller's boyish smile might charm a woman or inspire trust in a man, but Tom knew immediately that the smile was just an illusion. There was nothing of warmth or sincerity to back it up, and the eyes confirmed it. They were the eyes of a killer: worse, they were the eyes of a man who took *pleasure* in the act of killing.

This fact was confirmed by the

notches on the grips of the .45. Not too many — yet. But before long those grips would be fairly crosshatched with them, if this kid had his way.

Tom said mildly, 'Don't know anyone named Trigger.'

'No?'

'No. My name's Reese, boy. *Mister* Reese.'

The youth smiled, and as Tom had guessed, his face immediately became that of a seemingly pleasant young man. Still smiling, the youth said, 'Me, I'm Jim Tate.'

Tom drew a cautious breath. 'What can I do for you, son?'

'Isn't my name answer enough?'

'Afraid not.'

'Then you're a damn' liar, *Mister* Reese. You've heard the name before, 'cept back then, it was my pa who wore it. Remember *now* . . . Trigger? Brokaw, Kansas? Ten years ago?'

For a moment it was on the tip of Tom's tongue to say he didn't know what the kid was talking about, but he'd never been much for lying, and saw no point in starting now.

'Your pa was a rustler, Jim,' he said. 'A rustler, a thief and a bad man. I know that don't make it right, but that's the way it was.'

'He was everythin' you say,' Tate agreed. 'But for all that he was still my *pa*. That's all that matters to me.'

Slowly, carefully, Tom came out from between shelves stacked high with cloth and airtights. He was a tall, lean man a nudge past fifty, with a long, lean face and mild hazel eyes. Outside, the afternoon had turned a hazy, powdery blue. Cold wind made the door rattle in its frame, and sent loose dust swirling down the center of Main.

He said, 'So you figure to kill the man who killed your pa, is that it? You call me out, we face each other the way your pa and me faced each other all them years ago, then you shoot me down and that makes everything right again?'

'It makes it right for *me*,' Tate allowed.

'Well, I'm sorry to disappoint you,

Jim, but even if I still carried a gun — which, as you can see, I don't — all you'd get out of it is a pine box.'

Tate smirked. 'You're mighty sure of yourself, ain't you, Trigger? For a man who hung his gun up right after he killed my pa, I mean.'

'There's some things you never forget,' said Tom, adding with a bitterness he couldn't quite hide, 'How to kill a man's one of 'em.'

'Well, you might not *wear* a gun any-more,' said Tate, glancing idly around the store, 'but I know you still *got* one. Everyone's heard about how you hung yours up because you figgered your killin' days were over.'

He gave his own belt a slight twitch.

'Trouble is,' he went on, 'they're *not* over, Trigger. Not yet. So you better go take that pistol of yours down again, 'cause I'll be waitin' for you right out there at noon on Monday, an' I'll be expectin' you to use it.'

'I won't fight you, son,' Tom replied. 'Your pa broke the law and resisted arrest. He drew down on me an' I killed him. I didn't want to, but I didn't have any choice. He didn't *give* me the choice. So let's just leave it at that, all right?'

'Can't,' said Tate. 'It's been too long, Trigger. Everythin' I've ever done, every place I've ever been, every trick I've ever learned . . . it's all been leading to this, an' I'm not about to be cheated out of it now. So you be out there on that street at noon on Monday, an' you come armed, 'cause armed or not, I *will* kill you. Least you got *some* chance agin me if you wear your gun.'

His challenge delivered, he turned and walked out.

Alone again, Tom swore softly. Anger warred with a sudden, great tiredness in him. Wasn't it enough that he had to live each day haunted by the faces of all the men he'd ever killed in the line of duty? Didn't it count for anything that Tate's father had been the last in a long line — that he'd known he couldn't live with the weight of yet another death on his conscience, and done something about it?

When he'd tendered his resignation, the town council had reminded him that gunplay went with the job, as if that little fact might have somehow slipped his mind.

Well, there was no arguing with that. But neither was there any arguing with the feeling of dread that settled in him every time he saw how each new confrontation was going to end up; when the only outcome was to draw, aim and kill your opponent before he drew, aimed and killed *you*.

Besides, there was something else behind his decision.

In all his years as a peace officer, he'd never once considered the importance of luck. He'd always been handy with a gun, and was good at what he did. But that fight with Jim Tate's father . . . it had been such a close-run thing that he'd started to wonder if, just sometimes, luck *did* play its part.

If that was true, then the next time he

found himself facing a man wearing a gun he was intent on using, it might take nothing more than a simple distraction, or a momentary lapse in concentration, for it to end up being Tom Reese — 'Trigger Tom', as they'd taken to calling him by then — sprawled dead in the dirt.

This too had been behind his decision to quit, and he'd hated himself for the cowardly foolishness of it. But the look of relief on Jenny's face when he got home that night and told her the news was all the confirmation he'd needed to know that it had been the right thing to do. The old Tom Reese — *Trigger* Tom Reese — had vanished that night, and been replaced by a new one: a man who was happy just to run his store and watch his only son grow to manhood, and live out the rest of his days with the wife he adored here in this anonymous little town.

Until now.

He turned out the oil lamps he'd been forced to light against the overcast day, then exchanged his apron for his black suit jacket. Finally he locked up and hurried along the boardwalk, more or less the only soul abroad on this wintry Montana afternoon.

Chin tucked in against the biting wind, safe in the knowledge that if Jim Tate wanted to gun him down it would be face to face and not from ambush, he made his way up to the marshal's office.

Inside, Milt Garraway was reading a *Beadle's Dime Novel*. He'd had to light a lamp against the early darkness, too, and his office was warm as toast from the fire glowing in the iron belly of his Pilot No. 55 heater.

'Hello, Tom!' he greeted as he looked up. 'Finished early today?'

'This weather's keeping folks home.'

For a moment he warmed his hands at the pot-bellied heater. Then, 'Milt . . . does the name *Tate* mean anything to you? Jim Tate?'

The marshal thought about it. He was about ten years Tom's junior, with a tough, weathered face and a sand-colored mustache he seldom thought to trim. 'I seem to recollect a kid of that name stirrin' up trouble down in Arkansas. Killed a couple of men over cards, or maybe it was a woman.' He paused briefly, as something else occurred to him. 'Kid had an old man wasn't up to much.'

'I know about the old man,' said Tom. 'It was me who killed him.'

The marshal's brows notched high. 'That a fact? And this kid — ?'

'He's here, Milt. Spoke to him not ten minutes ago. He's called me out. Wants to face me out on Main, day after tomorrow.'

'What did you tell him?'

'What do you *think* I told him? I said his pa didn't give me much choice about it, that I didn't have any quarrel with him — the boy himself, I mean — and to leave me alone.'

'And?'

'I could've saved my breath. He's not backing off for anything.'

The marshal pushed up from behind

his paper-littered desk. 'Then I guess I better go look him up an' run him out of town.'

'No,' said Tom. 'I'll deal with it.'

Garraway shot him a keen glance. 'You're not fixin' to take up that hangin' gun of yours again, are you?'

'I don't know *what* I'm gonna do, yet,' Tom replied honestly. 'But it's my problem, Milt. I guess that's really why I stopped by — to tell you to stay away from him. He's poison.'

'All the more reason for me to post him out of town.'

'It wouldn't work. He's not gonna be denied, Milt. Not at any price.'

'Then where does that leave us?'

'Like I say, you keep your distance. He's my problem.'

'Your problems are mine, Tom. I'm the law around here, remember? It's things like this you folks pay me to handle.'

For the first time, Tom allowed himself a grim smile. 'All right,' he said. 'I'll put it another way. I'm *asking* you, friend to friend, not to get involved. I'll deal with it . . . somehow.'

Milt didn't like it, but they'd known each other long enough that he knew he had to respect it. 'All right,' he said grudgingly. 'But if you *do* decide to go out there on Monday and face him, you won't go out there alone. I'll be around, but I won't take a hand in it unless I feel I have to. Fair enough?'

It was, Tom knew, the best he could hope for. 'Fair enough. 'Preciate it, Milt.'

With that settled, he left the office and turned his steps toward home.

* * *

That morning, he and Jenny had quarreled for the first time he could remember. The argument had been over the future of their son, Ben. Tom had suggested that they might eventually send him east to learn law — a subject in which he'd often expressed interest — but the notion hadn't sat well with Jenny. She'd always been overprotective of the boy, and though she'd never come right out and said it, she hated the thought that he might one day grow up and leave home.

'You've got to let him go sooner or later,' he'd said. 'He's already fourteen and he hates it like hell when you coddle him — '

'I *don't* coddle him.'

'Well, that's how it looks to me, sometimes,' Tom replied. 'Any case, he learns law, he's got himself a darn good profession. It'll set him up as a man to respect in a town.'

'He can earn just as much respect if he stays here and eventually takes over the store.'

He'd cocked his head at her, as if seeing her for the first time. 'Is that what you really want for him? To become just another storekeeper, when he could be so much *more*? Just so you can keep him where you can see him?'

Her face had paled at that, and her green eyes had grown large. 'How dare you say that! I only want what's best for Ben!'

'All right — if you mean that, I'll tell

you what we'll do. We'll let *him* choose, when the time comes. Go out into the world and make something of himself, or stay home, afraid to do anything in case it breaks his momma's heart.'

She'd slapped him then. He'd seen it coming and made no attempt to dodge it, figuring that it would do her more good to get all the anger — yes, *and* guilt — out of her system. And she was *filled* with guilt, he could tell, because she had recognized the truth in his accusation, and try as she might to deny it, she couldn't.

Now Tom wondered if the argument had tormented Jenny throughout the day as much as it had him. Probably. But there was one way to know for sure whether or not she'd decided to make her peace with him. If baked hash were on the menu tonight, he'd know he'd been forgiven. He'd been a lover of beef hash all his life, it was his favorite, and Jenny knew it.

He went around the little clapboard house on Second Street so that he could enter through the kitchen. As he approached the back door the smell of kid pie and boiled potatoes came to his nostrils.

He grimaced. He *hadn't* been forgiven yet, then. And the mood he was in right then, he couldn't help wondering if he ever would be.

★   ★   ★

Later, as they were eating, Jenny said, 'I saw a stranger in town earlier today. Nice young boy. Raised his hat to me and smiled.'

She'd said it more to break the uncomfortable silence than anything else.

Tom looked at her with his fork halfway to his mouth. 'Curly blond hair?' he asked carefully.

'You saw him, too?' she asked. 'I hope he figures on staying a while. We've got more than our share of cowhands forever getting drunk and raising Cain. We could use someone with a few manners.'

'Hey,' said Ben, 'that sounds like the feller who was showin' us those tricks.'

'What tricks?' Tom asked sharply.

Ben shared his father's long, lean build, but his coloring was all Jenny's — eyes as green as meadow grass, hair the color of sea-washed sand on a Californian beach.

'Tricks with a gun,' the boy replied. 'A bunch of us was down the street and he stopped and spoke to us. Asked us our names — way he looked at me, seemed like he'd already heard mine. Then he showed us the tricks.'

'What tricks?' Tom repeated.

'There was one he called the Road Agent spin. Spun his gun by one finger in the trigger guard. Real fast. And then he showed us what he called the border shift. Threw the gun from one hand to the other and caught it real neat. Said you needed two guns to do it proper. Pa, could you — ?'

'Only one thing a gun's good for, Ben,' Tom snapped. 'And it's *not* for showing off with.'

Jenny gave him a tight-lipped glare. 'Oh, don't be so stuffy! He shouldn't have been fooling around with a gun, I grant you, but I doubt that he meant any harm by it.'

Before he could stop himself Tom said, 'And what would *you* know about it?'

Her eyes came up to his face. They were large and uncharacteristically cold. Softly, stiffly, she said, 'You will never take that tone with me again, if you please.'

He sagged. 'I'm sorry. I didn't mean for it to come out like — '

'Pa,' interrupted Ben. 'Tell us again about what it was like when *you* wore a badge. Plenty shootin' then, I bet.'

Instinctively Tom threw a long look at the holstered gun hanging from the hook to one side of the fireplace. It was a heavy, long-barreled .36 Navy Colt.

'*Shooting*, not *shootin*',' Jenny corrected the boy.

'Sure, Ma,' the boy said absently. 'But, Pa — '

'In any case,' Jenny continued, talking over him, 'tricks are all guns are good for, these days. The days when men settled their differences by shooting each other are *long* past. The country is finally getting itself civilized.'

'I *wish*,' Tom murmured, and went back to eating.

But once again he flicked a guarded look at the hanging gun, and this time he wondered how well he could still use it.

* * *

Jim Tate attended church services on Sunday morning. He made sure to catch Tom's eye — as if Tom was likely to miss him — and doffed his hat to Jenny, who was as impressed with his manners as she had been the first time she saw him.

The walk to church had been unusually silent, the rift between husband and wife still very much in evidence. So Tom was almost relieved when Milt Garraway stopped him after services and asked if he could have a private word.

'Sure,' he replied. And then, to Jenny and Ben, 'You two go on ahead. I'll catch you up.'

When they were out of earshot, Milt said, 'It's not too late, you know. I can take him right here, right now. Tell him to get out of town, that he's an undesirable, and if he shows his face again — '

Tom shook his head. 'No. We'll play this thing out to the finish. He won't let it go any way else.'

Milt's mouth thinned. 'Are you sure that's a good idea? Christ, man, you look awful.'

'Thanks,' Tom replied sourly. But there was no surprise in that. He'd hardly slept a wink the night before, and doubted he'd sleep much tonight, either.

'I just mean . . . look, no one'd think any worse of you if you left this to me — '

'I know. But *I* would.'

'Even if it means — '

The marshal bit off abruptly.

'Even if it means *what*?' Tom prodded.

'Nothin'.'

Tom let it go, but he knew what Milt had come so close to saying. *Even if it means turning your wife into a widow? Even if it means depriving Ben of his pa at just the age when a boy needs his pa the most?*

'It'll work out, Milt,' he said.

And it *would* work out.

There was just no telling which way, yet.

★　★　★

Tate was waiting for him when he arrived at the store early the following morning. It was another dull day, with a raw, insistent wind shunting clouds the color of bruises across the sky.

'Almost time, Trigger,' he grinned when Tom was close enough.

Bundled up against the cold, Tom sighed. 'I *really* don't want to fight you, son. There's no call for it. You could still back off, we could each go our separate ways and no harm done.'

'Just be out here at noon,' Tate replied, 'an' come armed. 'Cause armed or not, you and me are gonna finish this thing.'

Tom looked into the young killer's eyes. There was nothing in them but anticipation and confidence. He had no doubt that when the time came, he would win the contest between them. Tom, by contrast, was riddled with doubt. It had been so long — more than enough time for a man to slow down, get rusty —

Then Tate turned and sauntered away, and Tom slowly, quietly unbuttoned his overcoat, gently brushed back one fold to reveal the long-barreled Navy .36 he now wore at his hip.

He could end it now. He could draw his Colt and put a bullet in each of Tate's shoulders, so that the kid would never again be worth a damn in a fight. Or he could just finish him altogether with a bullet in the back.

But no. He could no more do that than let Milt handle the problem for him.

Instead he turned away from the departing youth and unlocked the store with a hand that trembled.

★ ★ ★

As they'd prepared for bed the night before, Jenny had finally broken her day-long silence.

'Is that what you *really* think?' she'd asked sharply. 'That I coddle Ben?'

He'd been in no mood to discuss the matter, but could hardly refuse to answer such a direct question. 'Honestly?' he said tiredly. 'Yes, I do.'

'Well, you couldn't be more wrong,' she informed him. 'I may *care* for him, but I certainly don't *coddle* him.'

'All right,' he said. 'Maybe I *was* wrong.'

'You *say* that,' she said, 'but you don't *believe* it.'

'No, I guess I don't. Because *caring* is

when you do something for the good of someone *else. Coddling's* what you do when you want to indulge *yourself.*'

'I resent that, Tom Reese.'

'I can't help that. You asked me and I told you.'

She slid into bed, turned onto her side, away from him. 'I only want what's best for Ben.'

'If you say so.'

'Don't you believe me?'

'Do you believe *yourself*?'

She turned and sat up again. 'You — ' And then, 'Where are you going?'

'Downstairs,' he said from the doorway. 'I don't feel much like sleeping right now.'

He'd spent the night in a fireside chair, wrapped in a blanket, not sleeping, just thinking. Thinking that if today turned out to be his last day, he didn't want to leave any ill feeling between them.

While it was still dark, he climbed the stairs and let himself back into the bedroom. He stood there for a while, listening to the irregular rhythm of Jenny's troubled sleep and decided against waking her. Instead he murmured, 'You're a good woman, Jen, and I love you.'

Then he turned and left the room, went into the kitchen and took down the hanging gun.

★ ★ ★

Outside, the weather remained raw, and because of that trade was pretty much nonexistent. Still, that was fine with Tom. The solitude gave him a chance to think, to plan, to retreat to the stock room and try to regain something of the speed and dexterity he'd lost over the years.

But his draw, when he made it, was a clumsy thing, slow, awkward, with nerves playing their part to make it even worse.

He took the Colt apart, cleaned it, reassembled it, dry-fired it a few times and then reloaded it with fresh rounds.

As he worked, his eyes constantly strayed to the clock on the wall, but time seemed to pass slow as molasses.

To make things worse, he lived every second of that morning with the fear that Jenny might suddenly glance up from this chore or that, and notice that the gun and belt were missing. If he could just get through the confrontation to come then he would tell her everything . . . or Milt Johnson would, if Tate proved to be the better man.

That made him think about luck again.

Part of him believed that a man made his own. But another part reminded him just how easily a man's life could turn on chance. He thought about Jenny, about Ben, about life in general — even, God help him, about beef hash.

And then, right out of the blue —

'Trigger!'

It was noon.

He flinched, suddenly aware that he'd been lost in thought. As he pushed himself up off the counter against which he'd been leaning, he saw Tate beyond the store's dusty windows, standing in the center of the street, facing him with legs spread for balance and hands hanging loose at his sides, fingers flexing in anticipation of the killing to come.

And the sonofabitch was *smiling* at him.

With a sense almost of unreality, Tom came around the counter, fighting to clear his mind of everything save the need to focus absolutely on what had to be done.

He crossed the store like a condemned man, opened the door. The wind almost tore the handle from his grasp. His breathing was shallow now, but his heart was racing.

He looked out at Tate and saw surprise in his expression — the kid had more or less convinced himself that Tom wouldn't face him — and then the surprise was replaced by eagerness, and Tom wondered if that might be his undoing.

He told himself, *Easy now, easy*

. . . just concentrate on what needs to be done . . .

Up on the far boardwalk and about twenty yards to the left, he saw Milt Garraway, standing with long gun held white-knuckled athwart his chest.

Then Tom stepped down off the boardwalk, into the street. Now no more than thirty feet separated him from his opponent. With a confidence he didn't feel he called, 'Last chance, Jim.'

Tate's lips twitched.

'For *you*,' he called back.

'All right,' Tom said, tone flat now. 'Make your play.'

And that was when Jenny screamed from someplace behind him, '*Tom!*'

He didn't even have the chance to curse, could only think in that vital sliver of a second that here it was, the momentary distraction he had come to fear — and it had been provided by his own wife —

Trying to recover his concentration, he saw Tate's right hand blur across his belly, his fingers claw at the notched grips of his .45, and he was faster than Tom had ever thought possible.

But his own hand was also moving, swooping toward the butt of the hanging gun, and then it was coming up in his right fist, and his left hand was sweeping across to fan the hammer —

There came the crash of a shot and something sledgehammered him in the shoulder. He lurched backwards, face screwed tight, a jumble of thoughts cascading through his mind: *Faster . . . he was faster . . . he got me . . . I didn't want Jenny to see this . . .*

He collapsed to his knees, looked at Tate through pain-glazed eyes, saw the kid coming closer, taking his time now, basking in the moment he'd waited so long to experience . . .

Again Jenny screamed, '*Tom!*'

Milt Garraway came down into the street, started to slap the stock of his Winchester to his shoulder —

And finally, Tom brought his .36 up again even though it seemed to weigh a ton, and somehow he found the strength to fan the hammer, once, twice —

Both bullets punched Jim Tate smack in the center of the chest. He folded over and his gray Stetson fell from his golden curls and rolled away. Tate hung there for a stretched second, teetering, the gun in his hand pointing toward the dirt. Then he tried to straighten up again and Tom, light-headed now, fading, fading, shot him a third time.

Jim Tate staggered, swayed, collapsed. And so did Tom.

* * *

As he slowly regained consciousness, he realized he was in his own home, in his own bed, and though his shoulder-wound ached like a bitch it had obviously been tended. He'd been bandaged tight and neatly, and the sickly scent of ether on the air told him that Doc Wheatley had been here, operated on him and removed the bullet.

He turned his head against the pillow and saw Jenny and Ben watching him anxiously from the other side of the bed. They both looked like they'd been crying. Now, as he blinked and tried to swallow with a throat that was dry as a bone, they came to him in a rush.

'*Dad!*' said Ben, his voice catching. '*Dad, we thought — !*'

'Never mind what we thought,' Jenny interrupted. She took Tom's right hand, squeezed it, and fresh tears shone in her eyes. 'Ben,' she managed. 'G-go fetch your father a glass of water.'

Ben's expression said he wanted to stay right where he was, but he wanted to make himself useful, too, so he went grudgingly but without complaint.

As he left the room, Jenny said, her voice thick with emotion, 'Milt . . . Milt told us all about it. About that . . . *boy*, I mean. Tom, why didn't you tell me — ?'

Dazed, Tom closed his eyes. 'Seems to me we . . . had other things on our mind . . . at the time.'

Waving that aside she continued, 'When I saw that you'd taken down the gun . . . oh, Tom, I thought you might do something foolish — '

'It *was* foolish,' he managed wearily. 'Like you said, the days when men settle their differences by shooting each other are long past.'

'Well,' she said, 'I was wrong about that.'

He looked up at her. 'And maybe *I* was wrong . . . too. Maybe I *did* get . . . coddling mixed up with caring.'

'No,' she said. 'You were right, and we both know it. It's just that Ben . . . he's all we have, Tom. And — '

'And that's all the more . . . reason to let him run free,' he told her. 'To let life . . . toughen him up and prepare him for the future, Jen. It doesn't mean you have to . . . stop loving him. But it *does* mean you can give him his freedom, and there's nothing more precious than that.'

She nodded. 'That's the way it'll be from now on,' she promised. And then, tearfully, 'Oh, Tom, I've hated the past few days.'

'Not as much as I have,' he returned wryly. 'Where's the gun?'

'Back on its hook beside the fireplace,' she said. 'Where it belongs.'

The door opened and Ben came in, carrying a glass of water in both hands.

'Get on up here, boy,' said Tom, patting the mattress with his good hand. 'Help me slake this darn' thirst.'

Ben was happy to oblige, gently tilting the glass to his lips.

'Now you rest up,' Jenny said, moving to the door. 'You lost a lot of blood out there, Tom. Doc says we've got to build you up again.'

He smiled at her. 'I can think of one sure way to do that,' he said softly.

'So do I,' she said. 'That's why I'm fixing beef hash for supper.'

Comanche Reckoning

Link Dayton was out back, chopping wood, when he heard the young boy shout, 'Rider comin', Pa!'

He was a bulky man forty summers old, with a mess of black hair spilling from beneath his loose-brimmed hat and a shaggy black beard that covered a square and stubborn jaw. He sunk the axe into the stump nearby, straightened to his full six feet two, wiped his over-large hands on the bib of his stained coveralls and headed for the house.

Mary — a tired, prematurely aged woman with auburn hair pulled back in a bun — was waiting for him when he entered the parlor. Dayton ignored her as he took the old Burnside carbine down from the brackets over the hearth.

'Link — '

'Hush, woman.'

'But — '

He turned to face her then, and there was so much animation in his usually flat eyes that she fell silent.

'You know I can't be too careful,' he said quietly.

Back on the porch, with the long gun held ready across his barrel chest, he watched the rider come ever closer. Behind him, his home — a small, poorly maintained three-room dwelling built from rough-hewn logs — sat baking in the sun.

A moment later Timmy and the dogs came to join him.

'Go inside, son,' Dayton said softly.

Timmy was ten years old and favored his mother. He had a fine, delicate face that lacked Link's heavy brow and bitter twist of lip. His eyes were big and blue, his nose small and freckled.

'But — '

'Inside, I said!'

Dragging his heels, the boy reluctantly did as he was told. He didn't understand, Dayton told himself miserably. And who could blame him? Out here in the hard-scrabble land of the Panhandle, visitors were rare, and should have been welcome at any time. But they were never welcome on Dayton land. *Never*.

The only sounds now were the bleating of his sheep up on the north pasture, the clucking of the chickens pecking at the ground around the well, the closer buzz and whip of restless flies.

After a while, the rider trotted his dapple-gray gelding into the yard. Studying him closely, Dayton saw a man on the sundown side of thirty, with a battered face, cauliflowered ears and striking blue eyes. He wore a plain cotton work shirt beneath a wolfskin jacket, and creased cords over high-heeled, spurless cowman's boots. Dayton also saw that he wore his sidearm in a specially molded, low-strung holster.

The stranger tugged briefly at the brim of his tobacco-brown Stetson, a greeting Dayton acknowledged with a sharp nod.

'Somethin' I can do for you?' Dayton asked stiffly.

'Name's O'Brien,' said the man on

the dapple-gray. 'Mind if I climb down for a spell? Like to have a word.'

Dayton frowned. 'A word? What about?'

O'Brien said, 'Comanches.'

Dayton felt the blood drain from his face. 'Are you — ? Is this some kind of trick? Did Bohannan put you up to this? Is that it?'

O'Brien took his hat off and slapped it against his thigh. Beneath the harsh Texas sun, his close-cropped hair was the color of salt mixed with pepper. 'Who's Bohannan?' he asked.

Dayton worried at his lower lip, wondering who this man was and how far he could be trusted. Finally, feeling the eyes of his wife and son burning into his back from inside the house, he made a nervy gesture with the barrel of the rifle. 'Step down,' he muttered, adding grudgingly, 'I suppose you'll, ah, coffee an' cake with us?'

'Thanks.'

O'Brien followed Dayton into the house and through to the kitchen, where Mary was already standing at the copper-lined sink, filling the coffee pot with beans and water. Timmy, loitering by the back door, watched the newcomer with open curiosity.

Introductions made, the men took seats at the scrubbed pine table, where Dayton locked eyes with O'Brien and said, 'If Bohannan *did* send you here — '

'I'm here about *Comanches*, Dayton. I don't even know who Bohannan is.'

'Well, speak your piece, then,' said the shepherd.

O'Brien did.

'I cut their sign this morning, about ten miles south of here,' he reported. 'There's a bunch of 'em, fifteen, twenty. And from all the busted glass I found, I'd say someone's been selling 'em *bosa-pah*.'

Dayton looked blank.

'Firewater,' O'Brien explained.

'But — Christ, there hasn't been any trouble with the Comanches for years. I thought they were all further north.'

'So did I,' O'Brien replied. 'I was wrong.'

Dayton fell silent then, turning

O'Brien's words over in his mind. Finally, he licked his lips and said, 'Did . . . did it look like they was headed this way?'

O'Brien shrugged. 'No way of telling for sure where they'll end up,' he replied. Glancing at the sheep-dotted pasture beyond the small kitchen window, he asked, 'Do you run this place on your own?'

Dayton lost his far-away look momentarily. 'Me, my wife. The boy helps out. It's not a large spread, as you can see. This house, the barn, a couple of shelter pens.'

'Any neighbors who could send you a couple of their hands till this blows over?'

The shepherd's short, bitter laugh told O'Brien that he'd asked a foolish question. A mutton-puncher smack in the middle of cow-country could expect little in the way of help from his neighbors, and they both knew it.

'Better forget about that coffee, then.'

'Huh?'

'You folks'll be a heap safer in town, leastways for a night or two, and the sooner you get moving, the better. There's a town about twelve miles east of here, isn't there? Place called Kingfield? We'll ride in together, if you've a mind.'

'Mister, I ain't set foot off this spread in better'n twelve months, save to take my stock to market. I can't just up an' — '

'Maybe you didn't understand me,' O'Brien cut in. 'There's about twenty Comanche bucks somewheres out there right now, roaring drunk and spoiling for a fight. And drunk or sober, they don't come any meaner than the Comanches. Now, it could be that they won't touch anywhere near your spread. Could be that they'll sober up and ride on back to the reservation. Or it could be that they'll come here with blood in their eyes.'

Mary came forward at last. 'Link!'

'It *could* happen, Dayton.'

The shepherd turned his dark, flat eyes out to the scrubby pasture beyond the window. O'Brien watched his profile, the working of his jaw.

'I'm beholden to you for bringin' the news,' the big man said at length. 'But I reckon you can understand the position. We live a hard life out here, an' bein' a sheep farmer hasn't made it any easier. Oh, we get by — just — but we've had to learn to do without other folk. Reckon we'll do without 'em now.'

'But — '

'I couldn't just up stakes and leave this place, even if I wanted to,' Dayton argued. 'You think we'd be welcome in Kingfield? About as welcome as cholera! And anyway, I'd as soon take my chances with the Comanches as with Bohannan and them folks in town. At least I know where I stand with the Indians.'

O'Brien's lips compressed. 'Then you're a fool, Dayton — especially if those Comanches *do* come a-calling. A damn' fool.'

Still, Dayton wasn't the only damn' fool abroad that day. As he finished his coffee, O'Brien decided to do something pretty foolish himself.

'If you're sure you won't ride into Kingfield for the night, I reckon you could use an extra hand here, just to be on the safe side,' he said.

Dayton hesitated. 'Well, I'd have to think about it — '

'What is there to think about?' asked Mary. 'Link, if Mr. O'Brien's right, and those Indians *do* decide to come out this way — '

'They won't.'

'But if they did — '

Dayton slammed one big fist against the tabletop to silence her. 'All right, all right!' he snapped. To O'Brien he said, 'You can bed down in the barn.' And then, to Mary, 'Are you happy, now?'

★   ★   ★

Night came fast to the West Texas plains. By seven the land was ink-splashed with shadow and washed silver-gray by a hunter's moon.

After the evening meal — a thin rabbit stew — Mary took Timmy off to bed and the two men sat by the hearth, listening to the lonely wind outside.

'I apologize,' Dayton murmured at length. 'For earlier, I mean. An' I'm obliged to you, for stayin' over. If I seemed ungrateful, it's just that . . . well, we're not used to company, out here.'

'Just being neighborly is all,' O'Brien replied, taking out the makings.

Dayton snorted, said, 'Don't talk to me about neighbors.'

'You're talking about this feller Bohannan, I take it?'

'I am,' the big man said stiffly. 'Sumbitch owns one of the biggest cattle-outfits in the Panhandle, an' like most of his kind, he's got no time for sheep, nor the men who raise 'em. He always made it clear I wasn't welcome hereabouts, him more than any of the others. Even tried to buy me out about a year ago, just to be rid of me. Said in so many words that if I didn't accept his offer, I'd be sorry. But I got my pride, O'Brien. I told him to go to hell.'

'What did he say to that?'

'Nothing,' said Mary, coming back into the room. 'He didn't say a word, Mr. O'Brien, and he didn't do a thing. He just let it ride.'

'What she means,' Dayton amended, throwing his wife a murderous look, 'is that he ain't done anythin' *yet*. But it's only a matter of time. Man like Bohannan, he's used to gettin' his own way, an' if he don't get it . . . well, you'll see. One day he'll make his move agin me — only I'll be ready for him.'

'So now you know what Link does, besides raise sheep,' said Mary, her voice high, tired, edgy. 'He waits. For twelve months he's waited. And for twelve months we've shut ourselves away here, asking nothing, giving nothing — just waiting.'

An uncomfortable silence descended over the room, into which O'Brien ventured, 'Maybe you've called it wrong, then, Dayton. I mean, if this Bohannan was going to make a move against you, he'd have done it before this, wouldn't he?'

'That,' said Dayton, 'is just what he *wants* me to think.'

'Oh, for goodness' sake, Link,' said Mary, clearly exasperated. 'When will you — '

But before she could say more, O'Brien hissed, 'Turn that lamp down!'

As Mary did as he said, he crossed to the far corner of the room, where he'd left his Winchester. Snatching up the rifle, he levered a shell into the breech and opened the front door.

The excited yapping of the dogs in the barn across the yard came to him clearly as he strained his eyes to pierce the gloom. Dayton filled the doorway behind him, his wife at his side, her breathing soft and anxious.

'What is it, man?' Dayton whispered.

O'Brien was about to reply when they all heard it.

A gunshot.

'What — ?'

Another couple of gunshots punctured the chilly night air, and without taking his eyes off the moon-washed land ahead, O'Brien reached out, grabbed hold of Mary's arm and pushed her back inside the room. 'Get Timmy and the pair of you hunker right over there by the hearth,' he instructed. 'Make sure you stay low.'

The woman hurried away as a new sound carried through the darkness.

War cries.

'My God,' whispered Dayton.

A heartbeat later they saw him — a single rider painted silver by the moonlight, heading towards them at a flat-out gallop. He was slumped forward over the horse's neck, partly hidden by the animal's flying mane.

'White man,' O'Brien said tightly. He glanced briefly at Dayton. 'When he gets near enough, get him off that horse and inside. I'll give you as much cover as I can.'

'But — '

'Just do it, Dayton!'

O'Brien moved out onto the porch and brought the rifle up to his shoulder in one fluid motion. The rider was no more than a hundred feet away now, the air behind him full of sound. The war cries grew louder, more insistent.

There was another gunshot, two more. Over in the barn, the dogs were now going crazy.

Then the newcomer's sorrel was in the front yard and the rider, more dead than alive from the look of him, hauled back on the reins.

The horse skidded to a halt, flecked with foam, an explosion of dust flying up around its stiff legs. The rider groaned and fell out of the saddle just as a bristling of arrows struck the animal's hindquarters. The horse rose up, screamed, fell onto its side with enough force to shake the ground.

'*Now, Dayton!*'

The big man leapt out into the yard just as the knot of pursuing Comanches thundered into sight. He grabbed the wounded man under the arms and started dragging him back to the house as arrows sliced the air around him.

O'Brien clenched his teeth and let them have a volley of lead in return. The war cries got louder, angrier, but the Comanches reined in about seventy, eighty feet away, taken aback by the unexpected fusillade.

Without taking his eyes off the Indians, O'Brien quickly thumbed reloads into the long gun. Then, just as Dayton hauled the wounded man into the house, the Comanches surged forward again, and O'Brien straightened up, firing his rifle from the hip.

Another horse went down in a tangle, crushing its squat, bare-chested rider beneath it. More arrows hit the wall above his head. O'Brien backed up, emptied the Winchester into the confusion and then threw himself back inside the house.

Timmy stood in the far corner, watching everything through wide, scared eyes. The room was illuminated only by what little moonlight filtered through the windows, and the only sounds came from the agitated dogs in the barn.

O'Brien stood to one side of the window near the door, reloading his hot rifle again. Beside him, Dayton looked like he badly wanted someone to tell him what to do next. And down on her knees in the center of the room, Mary was turning the newcomer gently onto his back.

There was blood on the right shoulder of the man's plain cotton shirt, a lot of it.

'What are they doing?' Dayton asked in a whisper.

O'Brien shrugged. 'We surprised 'em,' he replied. 'So they've backed off to get a better look at us.'

And once they've done that, he thought, *and seen how weak we are, they'll hit us again.*

The wounded man moaned and Mary whispered something to quieten him down. 'Link,' she went on, 'help me get his shirt off, so's I can look at the wound.'

Dayton looked at O'Brien, who said, 'Go on. I'll keep watch here.'

Dayton crossed the room and knelt beside the wounded man. A moment later he let out a curse that made O'Brien turn sharply.

'What is it?'

Dayton's face was carved in grim lines as he looked up from the body. 'I *knew* we should've kept out of this!' he rasped. 'Now we're all gonna get ourselves killed, just on account of *this* worthless sonuver!'

O'Brien narrowed his eyes. 'What? What are you talking about?'

'This here's Pete Bohannan,' Dayton replied through gritted teeth. 'My worst enemy's God-damned *son*!'

★   ★   ★

Silence hung heavy in the room for a long five seconds, until the man on the floor, hearing his name mentioned, stirred briefly.

' — wh-where am I — ?'

Dayton straightened up quickly, backpedaled a couple of paces as if Pete Bohannan's words might burn him. But Mary stayed where she was, told him what he wanted to know as the boy — O'Brien saw now that he was barely seventeen years old — looked at each of them in turn. Then —

'*Indians!*' he cried. His chocolate-brown eyes were large, feverish. 'They — '

'Easy now,' O'Brien said quietly. He looked at Mary. 'Get him some water, ma'am, if you will.'

As Mary got to her feet, Dayton said, 'You stay right where you are.'

'Link?'

'This man's not welcome here,' he said.

Outside, the dogs were still barking furiously.

'Dayton — '

'He's a *Bohannan*, damn him!'

The shepherd looked down at the young man, whose sweaty face was crushed with pain. Mary looked at him too, then turned with a swish of skirts and went into the kitchen. Dayton watched her go, his mouth open slightly. He listened to the noises she made at the pump, filling a mug with water.

He seemed to deflate then, as if all the life had gone out of him. He stalked across the room, fists bunched, peered out into the night. Behind him, Mary re-entered the room, knelt by Bohannan and lifted his head carefully, so that he might drink.

Once he'd had his fill, he said, 'Obliged to you — ma'am.' In the darkness, his voice sounded more like that of a small, frightened child.

'What happened, Bohannan?' O'Brien asked over one shoulder.

The boy's eyes went wide again. 'Me, Curly Jackson an' Sid Wheeler — we . . . we'd spent the day huntin' up strays,' he breathed. 'Th-then, 'long about five-thirty or so, we decided to get on back to the ranch. But — but as we topped a ridge, we saw 'em — them Indians, 'bout twenty of 'em, down in the valley below. They'd butchered a yearlin' an' was cookin' 'er up.

'Well, straight off, ol' Curly pulls iron an' fires a couple shots over their heads. He was just aimin' to scare 'em off, but I guess they got the wrong idea an' thought we was after attackin' 'em. So they comes at us, an' Curly, he fires again, hits one of 'em this time.

'M-minute later, Curly took an arrow in the chest. He was — dead by the time me an' Sid turned tail an' lit out of there. Trouble was, them Comanches, they follered us, wouldn't quit — got Sid — hit me in the arm — '

He broke off with a sob.

After a while he asked, 'Are they still out there, mister?'

O'Brien said, 'Yeah.'

'And because of *you*,' Dayton cut in, fixing the boy with a cold stare, 'we're all gonna die.'

'Dayt — '

'You gonna tell me I'm wrong?' demanded the shepherd. 'You gonna tell me them Comanches would've come here even if he *hadn't* led 'em to us?'

'*Shhh!*'

Silence filled the room again, unbroken this time, and it was what they couldn't hear that made them go cold.

The dogs.

O'Brien turned to the window, brought the rifle up in readiness. He thought he saw a shadow moving out there beside the barn, but that could have been his imagination.

'Look alive, Dayton,' he rasped.

'They're coming back. Get your rifle and help yourself to Bohannan's Colt and ammunition. Timmy, you stay right where you are, you got that? Ma'am — '

He didn't get the chance to finish. At that moment a bullet shattered the window, and he had to dance back a step to avoid a shower of glass. Dayton called his wife's name, Bohannan's handgun all but lost in his big fist.

'We're all right, Link!'

Then they were charging across the yard, those warriors who had dismounted and crept as far as the barn, where they'd butchered the dogs, who might otherwise give them away. They came with bows and arrows, lances and rifles, and they were mostly small, thickset men with bare, muscular chests and bowlegs, whose faces were painted with the reds and blacks of war.

O'Brien stuck the rifle through the jagged hole in the window and fired twice. There was no time to take aim; he just had to rely on instinct. Out in the yard one of the Comanches stopped halfway through bringing his lance up and went over backwards, clutching his chest.

Then more gunshots peppered the front of the house. Glass smashed in the window on the other side of the door, and Dayton twisted away from it, slammed his back against the wall and cried out more in shock than anything else.

O'Brien pumped in another round, fired. One of the Indians on the porch, no more than four feet away, jerked and fell, his war cry turning into a death chant. But still they kept coming, a relentless tide.

'Dayton!' O'Brien roared above their war cries. 'Use that damn' gun!'

There wasn't time to say more. The attack was becoming too fierce. But part of his mind became aware of the high, short bark of Bohannan's Colt in the shepherd's fist.

The fighting may have lasted a minute more. It was difficult to tell, since time lost all meaning. But then, suddenly, the attack was over, and the surviving Comanches melted back into the night.

O'Brien let out his breath, listening as Mary told Timmy not to fret, that everything was going to be all right; to Bohannan groaning through clenched teeth; to the tight, difficult breathing of Dayton at the other window. He levered another bullet into the Winchester and wondered if they could possibly last out the night.

'Will they — will they be back, do you reckon?' Dayton asked after a while.

O'Brien nearly replied. But then he heard a noise at the back of the house that could have been the wind. Or —

He crossed the room fast, got into the kitchen just as the back door burst open with a splintering of wood. Behind him Mary screamed. Timmy yelled. Dayton shouted something unintelligible.

Three Comanches spilled into the room.

The leader was a short, stocky man

with a red-and-black painted face and long, greasy black hair. He brandished a long, sturdy-looking lance with a stone head above its decoration of feathers.

He yelled, '*Maywaykin, sata teja!*'

It was an insult-laden death-threat, and O'Brien let him have a bullet in the face by way of reply. The Comanche was thrown backwards into his two friends.

They howled in a mixture of surprise and rage, and O'Brien heard more yapping behind them. There were more of them out there, a lot more, more than he could possibly handle. But there was no time to consider the odds.

He shot the second brave in the chest, put another bullet there to make sure, then swung the rifle to cover the third Indian. This one wore red war paint and three black circles around his left eye.

'*Maywaykin!*' he cried, lifting his hatchet. 'I kill you!'

'Not tonight, you won't,' O'Brien replied — and shot him between the eyes.

He spent one stretched minute crouched in the kitchen doorway, waiting. Then, when it became apparent that the Comanches weren't going to follow the attack up, he dragged the dead bodies into the house, closed the back door and piled the corpses against it to help keep it shut.

By the time he returned to the parlor, Mary was down on her knees in the far corner, arms wrapped protectively around Timmy. Dayton was peering out into the night. Bohannan had dragged himself into a sitting position. He looked pale, tired, desperate. They all did.

O'Brien took out his Hunter and checked the time. It was, incredibly, only a little past eight. He crossed the room and checked the front yard through his shattered window. Two dead horses and three Comanches littered the hard-packed earth.

Six Comanches down here, he thought, and one Bohannan's friend Curly had shot earlier. Assuming that there had been twenty to begin with, that meant there were still thirteen of them out there now.

Unlucky for some.

A minute stretched into two, five, ten, an hour. Nothing stirred across the vast Texas plain. Mary washed the crust away from Bohannan's wound and bound it as best she could. Then she and Timmy huddled together and dozed.

'I think I see 'em comin' back,' Dayton whispered after a while.

O'Brien checked for himself. 'It's nothing.'

'I tell you I can see 'em! They — '

'It's nothing, Dayton!' O'Brien repeated sharply. 'Just calm down. That's the whole point of this little waiting game of theirs — to work on your nerves.'

Silence returned to the little ranch house.

After a while, Dayton pointed a thick finger at Bohannan. 'This is all down to you,' he muttered. 'Don't forget that. You got us into this. You're the one they're after. Hell, they'd probably leave us alone was we to hand you over to 'em.'

'Just try it,' O'Brien said quietly.

Another minute passed slowly, after which Bohannan said, 'Mister, can I ask you somethin'?'

'What?' Dayton growled impatiently.

'What is it you got against me?'

When Dayton made no reply, O'Brien prodded softly, 'Man asked you a question.'

The big man threw him a glare. 'What the hell would you know about it, anyway?'

O'Brien shrugged. 'I know that it's a hell of a thing to be a sheepman in the middle of cattle country. With no friends, and no neighbors worth a damn, what else can a man like that become, other than a loner? What else can he have inside him, except anger and resentment? But who do you resent more, Dayton? Who is it you're really angry at — your neighbors, or yourself?'

'What the hell's that supposed to mean?'

'It means that maybe you've been

fighting prejudice for so damn' long that you've come to see things the way other folks see 'em,' said O'Brien. 'To see yourself as something less than the man you are.'

'You callin' me a failure?' asked Dayton, his voice low, gruff.

'I'm calling you a proud man who'd sooner tough it out than move on and start over someplace else,' said O'Brien. 'I'm calling you a man with guts, Dayton. A man other men'd admire.'

'Well, all that pride, it sure got me a long way, didn't it?' asked the shepherd, his mouth pulling down at the corners.

'It got you this far,' countered O'Brien. 'It got you this place, this land, a couple hundred head of prime stock. A good wife and a fine son.'

Dayton laughed bitterly. 'Yeah, Mary and Tim. Just look what I've been able to do for *them*.'

The words came in a torrent then, and big man couldn't have stopped them even if he'd tried.

'You think this is the life I want for

my folks? You think I want to keep Mary stuck out here on her own, or the boy with no other kids to grow up around? But what the hell choice do I have? Bohannan'll make his move, soon or late, an' if I'm not ready for him, that's it. We won't even have what we got right now. So I have to fort up, wait — '

'Listen to yourself, Dayton. Bohannan this, Bohannan that! Christ, man, you've spent so long waiting for Bohannan to make his move that you've forgotten how to live any other way! You've spent twelve months waiting for a man you hardly know to make a move he's never going to make.' He shook his head, said gently, 'You're a man who's lost his way.'

Pete, hanging on every word, said quietly, 'He's right, mister. We got nothin' agin you, 'sides what your dang sheep do to the land. We hardly even *know* you.'

'So what's the answer?' Dayton snarled, firing the question at O'Brien. 'You tell me *that.*'

'I haven't got an answer. But getting away from this place every once in a while, going into town, mixing with your neighbors, getting to know them and letting them get to know you . . . hell, it's a start.'

He broke off then, as a series of sounds from the direction of the north pasture drifted in on the cool night air. The high, frightened bleating of sheep. A squeal. Silence. And then a cold, challenging war cry.

Dayton's face went slack.

'My sheep,' he murmured. 'They're butcherin' my sheep!'

Just as the bleating of another sheep came through the chilly night air, O'Brien caught a movement out in the front yard and brought his rifle up.

'Dayton, get away from the window!'

But it was too late. Even as O'Brien fired at the partially hidden Comanche, an arrow from the brave's bow shot through the shattered window and punched Dayton high in the back.

It was a flint-headed arrow with a barbed tip. The flint gave it greater shocking power when it hit and the barbed tip made it impossible to remove in a hurry without causing even greater damage. As it struck him, Dayton cried out, staggered, dropped Bohannan's Colt and hit the parlor floor face-first.

'*Link!*'

'*Pa!*'

Mary was across the room in an instant, tears hot against her rough skin. Timmy was there too, his small hands clenching and unclenching helplessly at his sides.

And suddenly, O'Brien was all that stood between them and the Comanches.

The Indians appeared as if from nowhere. From behind the bodies of the horses they came, from the shadows of the barn and the well. They seemed to rise up from the very earth itself, and as they raced toward the house, there looked to be a lot more than the thirteen O'Brien had figured on, although he knew that could not be so.

He drew a bead on the leading Comanche, tracked him a second, shifted the barrel of the Winchester slightly ahead of the target, then fired. The Comanche ran straight into the slug and it picked him up and threw him away like a leaf in a high wind.

Then they were up on the porch, and he heard them howling like demons as they threw themselves against the barred door, determined to get inside. He fired once into those Indians still chasing across the yard, missed, cursed, took a pace away from the window.

Bohannan was up on his feet now, left hand outstretched. 'Gimme your gun!' he yelled above the chaos.

O'Brien glanced over his shoulder, beyond the young cowboy. The bodies piled at the back door were spilling over in a human landslide. The back door was slowly being pushed open.

'*Damn!*'

He drew his Colt and tossed it to Bohannan. It slipped through the young man's fingers and hit the floor. Bohannan scooped it up, staggered as far as the kitchen doorway and triggered all five shots through the back door. There were a few yelps above the whoops, then the door stopped its inward swing.

'*I need more ammunition!*' Bohannan cried.

But a splintering of wood spun O'Brien back toward the front door. There was no time to thumb fresh rounds from his belt. The first Comanche came through the door and O'Brien blew him away with a bullet from the rifle. As the second came into the room O'Brien fired again, but the hammer clicked on empty. Before the brave could reach him, he up-ended the rifle and smashed the Indian's face with the stock.

A third Comanche burst into the room, then a fourth and a fifth. Those out back started pushing at the kitchen door again. O'Brien swung the rifle for all it was worth, showering the room with blood and teeth. Bohannan threw the Colt across the room, snatched up his own gun from where it had fallen beside Dayton and emptied it into the marauders. When that was empty he threw that at them, too.

The din was tremendous. Mary was

screaming, Timmy sobbing. A lean, dark-skinned warrior almost fell into the room, carrying a wicked-looking axe in one hand and a lance in the other. His black eyes glittered when they lit upon O'Brien. The brave's face creased in a war cry as he raised his axe for throwing.

Before he could strike, however, a bullet hit him in the back and slammed him flat against the parlor floor.

There was no time for surprise. O'Brien stayed exactly as he was, crouched in readiness, holding the Winchester as a club as more shots peppered the night.

The startled Comanches at the front of the house stopped yapping and spun around to see where the new threat was coming from. One brave hit the outside wall and spilled down off the porch, leaving a crimson smear behind him. Another one hit the ground about two seconds later.

Time seemed to suspend itself then, and all around them the night held its breath. Then, abruptly, the Comanches broke, turning tail to disappear into the darkness before they could suffer further casualties.

It took O'Brien a while to get his breath back, but then he crossed the corpse-strewn floor and made it to the doorway just as a group of riders thundered into the yard outside. It was difficult to tell just how many of them there were. He thought perhaps as many as ten. Half at least rode straight by, to continue the chase. The rest reined in, dismounted, looking with awe at the carnage that surrounded them.

For long moments then the night was as still as the grave.

Then they all heard the distant rattle of gunfire.

And after that died away O'Brien heard Mary weeping softly behind him.

He let the rifle drop to the floor, turned and stumbled to the woman. He knelt beside her, eased her fingers away from her husband's body. The room was dark, too dark to see properly, but he could feel Timmy's eyes upon him.

'You all right, Bohannan?' he asked over his shoulder. His voice was a husky, painful rasp.

'Y . . . yeah . . . '

'Get a lamp working, will you?'

Before Bohannan could do that, a new voice, deep and relieved, made itself heard.

'*Pete!*'

O'Brien looked up as Bohannan almost fell into the arms of a taller, older man. The newcomer had a large belly, wore a heavy woolen jacket and had thick gray sideburns that framed a sunned, seamed face. This, he told himself, must be Pete's father, the Bohannan he'd heard so much about today.

As he pulled his son closer to him, the rancher said, 'Charlie! Get some light in here!'

Bohannan's men filed into the room, and while one of them located and then re-lit the lamp, the rest dragged the dead Indians outside. The rancher held his son at arm's length, then indicated the boy's wound.

'Hurt bad?'

Pete attempted a shrug. 'It's okay. Mrs. Dayton here . . . she patched it up some.'

'God, but you had me worried!' Bohannan said with feeling. 'I'd just 'bout given up all hope on you when you an' the others didn't show up at the house. Then, when MacDonald found Curly an' Sid — '

Suddenly, and to his great surprise, O'Brien felt Dayton stir beneath his hand, and as light spread through the room, the shepherd turned his pale face toward the rancher.

Mary sucked in a deep, shocked breath. 'Link!'

Dayton's dull, bloodshot eyes remained fixed on Bohannan as he rasped, 'All right . . . you got what you came for . . . now get the hell off my land!'

Instead Bohannan came further into the room, and O'Brien backed away to allow him to kneel beside the shepherd.

'God, but you look a sorry state,

Dayton!' the rancher declared. 'But just hang on. Where doctorin's concerned, I got me one of the best. He'll fix you up in no time.'

If he'd had the strength, Dayton might have spat. 'Get out of here!' he repeated vehemently. 'I'd as soon die as be beholden to you!'

'I don't want your gratitude,' Bohannan replied grimly. 'Besides which, you got it the wrong way round. It's me who's beholden to *you*.'

'How'd you . . . figure that?'

'I can read the sign, man!' said Bohannan. 'My boy would've ended up dead meat if you hadn't taken him in when you did! Don't think I don't 'preciate that.'

'But — '

'That's about right, Pa,' said Pete Bohannan, coming over. His eyes met those of the shepherd. 'If Dayton here hadn't bought into it when he did, I'd be dead for sure by now.'

The rancher growled over his shoulder, 'Where in hell's Sam gone to? Man here needs some attention!'

Sam appeared a moment later. He was a big man with dark hair and a steerhorn mustache. When he took his coat off and rolled up his sleeves, muscles like knotted ropes showed in his arms, but when he cut Dayton's shirt away, his touch was amazingly gentle.

'Just lay still a while,' Bohannan instructed while the other man began his examination. 'An' don't worry 'bout a thing. You'll feel more'n a mite sore by the time Sam here's done with you, but a week or two in bed'll soon fix you up.'

Dayton's eyes went wide. 'I can't — '

'Yes, you can,' the rancher insisted. 'Much as it sticks in my craw to nurse sheep, I got a couple men who can keep things movin' along here till you're back in harness.'

Dayton's lips curled into a sneer. 'You'd . . . do that . . . for me?' he asked skeptically.

'Ayuh,' Bohannan replied with a nod. 'I'm obliged to you, Dayton. The boy

. . . he's all I got, since Phoebe passed away. If I lost him as well . . . '

He cleared his throat noisily, squared his shoulders again. 'I'll admit, you an' me ain't never seen eye to eye. You're an ornery cuss, an' I daresay you'd say as much for me. But there's not many men that'd do what you did for my boy, not an' put his own family at risk by tanglin' with them Indians. Makes me feel that maybe I've misjudged you, some. An' that bein' the case . . . I'd appreciate the chance to set things right between us.'

As Dayton looked up at him, something deep inside his eyes stirred, shifted and changed. He wasn't used to praise, respect, friendship, and he wasn't quite sure how to take it.

He strained to look up at O'Brien, who was holding a tearful Timmy in his arms some way away, while Mary busied herself helping Sam to prepare to remove the arrow. O'Brien gave the shepherd a tired smile of encouragement, and an almost imperceptible nod.

And at that, Dayton seemed to reach a decision.

'Think . . . maybe we both might've misjudged each other . . . Bohannan.'

And for the first time since O'Brien had met him, the big shepherd looked at peace.

Whether or not it would last, no man could say. But maybe this was the start O'Brien had talked about earlier. And if it was, then Dayton was going to swallow his pride — and seize it with both hands.

Stretch-Hemp Station

Walt Bevan came to with a low, drawn-out moan, awakened — as usual, these past few mornings — by a bad dream he'd sooner forget. He rolled over, saw by her absence that Nellie was already up and doing, and told himself blearily, *Well, that figures.* Nellie hadn't been sleeping much better'n him, just lately.

He lay there a moment longer, feeling old, addle-brained, and more than a mite desperate. Then, damned if he'd feel any sorrier for himself than he had to, he tossed back the rumpled sheet and threw his bowed legs over the edge of the tick mattress.

Finger brushing the fine white hair back off his sun-darkened forehead, he stepped into a pair of gray wool pants and thumbed wide brown suspenders up over his sloped shoulders. His boots came next, a sorry-looking pair of scuffed old stovepipes, and after that he went in search of his wife.

He knew he wouldn't find her indoors, so he didn't waste time searching the station. He just shuffled straight through the common room and out into the gloomy, pre-dawn yard beyond.

His home, Stretch-Hemp Station, straddled a rutted wagon-road set amid sandy flats and screwbean mesquite. The station itself, a single-story structure split in two by a covered dogtrot, was built from logs chinked with mud. The stable and sheds on the far side of the trail were constructed in like fashion.

As Walt appeared in the station doorway, a scrawny collie called Sam slunk over with his head held low. The dog, white through the chest and forelegs and black everywhere else, had sharp-pointed ears and inquisitive, black-patch eyes the color of tobacco. No longer sure how to take his previously amiable master, however, the animal halted a few feet away, offered a couple of wary tail-wags and then waited hopefully for a response that never came.

Nellie, Walt saw, was standing about thirty yards to his right, her work-worn fingers knitting absently as she contemplated the rim of a gentle slope that lifted skyward behind the station. The slope itself had been cleared of timber about twenty years earlier, partly to provide cheap, but by no means entirely suitable, material with which to build the place and partly to deny Indians — Comanches mostly, but every so often a few fractious Kiowa, Cheyenne, and Arapaho as well — the cover they needed to sneak up on it.

Now only one tree remained up there to crown a slope otherwise choked with cholla and greasewood, one single, gnarled post oak that stood thirty feet high. No one had ever told them why it had been spared when the construction team first set to work, and neither had they ever thought to ask. It just had.

Walt studied his wife pensively as the rising sun continued to sketch her in shades of red, ochre, and amethyst. In her late fifties now, and thus of an age with him, she had big hips and a generous bosom that her thin cotton dress was finding increasingly difficult to contain. A short woman, she wore her longish, iron-gray hair fixed in a knot at the back of her head.

Clearing his throat to let her know he was there, Walt went to join her with Sam trotting cautiously at his side. 'You all right?' he asked when he was close enough.

'Just thinkin',' she replied vaguely.

'Well, don't,' he advised. 'All the thinkin' in the world won't change things.'

'No,' she agreed. 'But . . . ' Breaking off, she studied him closely through troubled brown eyes, then half-whispered, 'How long you suppose we can go on like this, Walt?'

He knew exactly what she meant, of course, but some belligerent streak made him demand, 'Like what?'

'How long can we keep goin' 'til we break?'

'Long as we have to, I guess,' he replied stubbornly.

He was about to say more when he realized that Sam had started up the hill, headed for the post oak, and all at once his fists clenched and he yelled, '*Sam!*' with such force that Nellie flinched and Sam spun around fast and immediately slunk back down to join them, his brushy tail tucking beneath his body.

'Goddamn you, dog!' Walt snarled.

Watching him, and seeing only a stranger where her husband used to be, Nellie said quietly, 'I'll start breakfast.'

As she walked past him, he felt an urge to reach out and tell her he was sorry, that he loved her, that nothing was ever going to come between them, he promised. There were a thousand and one things he wanted to say in that one brief moment, but then she was gone, and it was too late to say any of them.

While Nellie got the place cleaned up and ready for the noonday halt, Walt went over to the stable and turned the horses out into the corral. He swept out the stalls and topped up the troughs, then found some shade and, as the morning progressed, tried to concentrate on mending harness.

But his mind just wasn't on it. As the sun tried its best to bake the little home station he'd managed these past fifteen years, his eyes returned time and again to the lone post oak. As the day wore on, its shadow would crawl down the slope like a restless stain until it almost touched the station itself, and he would see it, as he had seen it for days now, more like the shadow of an accusing finger.

'Course, back when they'd first moved out here, the place had been named for that very tree. Post Oak Station. Forty miles from the swing station at High Point and closer to sixty from Coperas.

Upwards of twenty coaches a week had passed through here back then, going from Coperas to Fort Stockton and back again. But then the railroads had linked up and the stage lines, especially the smaller ones, had found it almost impossible to compete.

So economies had been made. The less-profitable routes were axed. Stock tenders quit and never got replaced. And many of the more isolated swing stations were abandoned altogether.

But Post Oak Station, standing as it did midway between the start and the end of the line, had always stayed open for business.

Not that they called it Post Oak Station anymore. They hadn't called it that in twelve years. Nowadays it was known as Stretch-Hemp Station, and with good reason.

It had all started with the arrival of the afternoon stage from Canfield: better'n two thousand pounds of bright red Concord weighed down with baggage, mail and passengers, running twenty minutes late and leaving a rising plume of back-lit yellow dust in its wake.

While Walt set to work unhitching the lathered team, the passengers had climbed down to stretch their legs and then disappear into the station for a cup or two of Nellie's strong coffee and a bite to eat. There was a merchant, he remembered, a couple of chamber pot and pin drummers, two women, a soldier whose single bar identified him as a lieutenant, and a stocky cowboy in need of a shave.

As always, Walt's son, Luke — a tall, slim boy with unruly sand-colored hair and his old man's long, pared-down features — had been there to walk the sweating horses 'til their breathing calmed, leaving Walt himself to back their replacements into the traces and set to work drawing the cinches firm.

He'd been doing that when the posse rode in.

There were seven of them sitting saddle behind the eighth — townsmen mostly, saloon workers, a blacksmith's apprentice, and a couple or three cowboys, each one hot, dusty, and somber-looking. Without taking his green eyes off the station, the rail-thin fifty-year-old at their head indicated the star pinned to the front of his leather vest and said, 'Amos Drake, Sheriff of Canfield.'

Walt had frowned. 'Help you, Sheriff?'

Drake dismounted and the men behind him did likewise, a few hitching expectantly at their hurriedly donned belt guns. Without bothering to reply, the lawman pushed past Walt and strode toward the station with the posse-men following eagerly at his heels, and Walt fell into step beside him, ducking as they went through the low doorway and into the common room beyond.

The driver, messenger, and passengers were seated on benches either side of a long sawbuck table. They'd been working their way through corned beef, carrots, and mashed potatoes when the posse arrived. Now the meal lay forgotten and all heads had turned enquiringly.

'Charlie Altman,' said Drake, pulling to a halt. 'Best you come quietly, now.

You're under arrest.'

A fleeting moment of shock followed the announcement. Then one of the two drummers climbed to his feet and said, 'What? What am I supposed to've done?'

'You killed a woman named Annie Redhead,' snapped Drake.

The drummer's dark eyes suddenly bulged. 'She's dead?' he murmured before he could stop himself. Then, defensively, 'I didn't kill anyone! The damned cocotte tried to steal my wallet, so I slapped her, that's all!'

'You beat her to death when she refused to give you your money back,' Drake countered grimly. 'That's the story she told as she lay dyin', an' be she sportin' girl or no, we don't stand to see our women treated that way!'

Sensing the strength of feeling among the men who'd come to arrest him, Altman hurriedly reached into the folds of his black coat and tore out a gun. 'Stay back, the lot of you!' he cried. 'I mean it!'

Nellie, framed in the kitchen doorway,

172

put a fist to her mouth. 'These men at my back are mad enough at you as it is,' growled Drake. 'Put up that smoke-wheel before you make things worse.'

Good as it was, however, Altman ignored the advice. 'Stay back, I said! And you, station-keeper! Go saddle me a horse! Now!'

'Nope,' said Drake, before Walt could move. 'You're comin' with us, Altman, so you just put up that pistol, or so help me I'll come over there and take it away from you myself.'

'It'll be the last thing you ever try!' warned Altman.

Undaunted, Drake started to advance on him, one hand outstretched. 'I'll take the gun,' he said softly.

'You'll take one end of it!' screamed the drummer.

And then, from a distance of no more than three feet, he shot Drake twice in the chest.

The bullets folded Drake in half and flung him to the dirt floor. One of the women screamed, there was a sudden ripple of movement that ceased almost as soon as it started, and then there was only silence, save for the sheriff's soft moans as the life seeped out of him.

Altman himself stumbled back a pace, apparently stunned by what he'd done. He seemed unable to take his eyes off the dying man — until the lieutenant suddenly sprang up and made a grab for him. He twisted then, brought the gun up and fired again, and the lieutenant cried out and went down clutching his hip.

One of the posse-men yelled, '*Get him!*' and after that all hell broke loose. Women screamed, men yelled, Walt started shouting for them to wait, to stop, and Altman, sending a warning shot into the ceiling, bawled at them to get back or else.

His words fell on deaf ears, though, and within seconds they were upon him and tearing the gun from his fist.

Squealing now, Altman lashed out blindly, broke one man's nose, kicked another between the legs, and knocked some teeth out for a third. But then they had him by the arms and were dragging him through the door, leaving Nellie to tend the wounded soldier and Walt to close the dead sheriff's staring eyes.

By the time Walt joined them outside, one of the posse-men had produced a length of good, strong hemp and was jabbing a finger at the post oak from which the station had taken its name.

Oh Lord, Walt remembered thinking. *They're gonna hang him*.

And in a way, who could blame them? This man had killed a woman in their town. He'd just killed the man to whom they'd entrusted their law and order. He'd injured three of their number and he'd damn-near killed the soldier-boy. So these hot, dusty, saddle-sore men were fired-up and hungry for vengeance, and what was right and what was wrong never came into it.

Still, even as they slammed a crude noose down over Altman's head, Walt begged them to reconsider. This wouldn't be justice, he argued, it'd be murder.

Better to let the law take its course, surely?

But there was no reasoning with them, and shoving him aside, the posse-men drew the hemp collar tight and dragged Altman through Nellie's flower garden, trampling her yellow coneflowers and just-blooming horsemint underfoot, then on up the brushy slope toward the tree, and young Luke, still standing in the corral with the gunfire-spooked horses milling around him, saw and heard it all.

He heard Altman scream curses at his captors and then, just as quickly, start begging them for mercy. He saw them fling the rope over the stoutest branch and then take up the slack on the loose end. He saw Altman's legs leave the ground as he was jerked higher, higher, higher, and watched as Altman's fingers clawed desperately to keep the hemp from biting any deeper into his throat.

Luke saw, too, the change that came into Altman when he finally realized that this was it, that he was actually going to die and that this was going to be the manner of his passing. He saw the last furious, frantic kicking of his legs, the gradual, inexorable darkening of his face from pink to plum and then to near-black, and finally he saw the drummer's hands flop to his sides, his legs stop their thrashing and settle to a weird, spastic quivering.

Luke saw and heard all that, and he was just twelve years old.

★ ★ ★

Walt sighed at the memory.

In the days, weeks, months, and years that followed, Nellie often woke up nights claiming to hear a sound drifting down from the post oak like stretched hemp creaking gently back and forth. Walt had always told her it was her imagination, and said pretty much the same thing whenever she talked about the station being cursed.

After all, things hadn't turned out so

bad, had they? For a start, that soldier-boy had lived, was a captain now, last he'd heard, and he hadn't even been left with as much as a limp. Pretty darn' good for a man who'd been shot in the hip.

And comes to that, what about Luke?

Oh, the events of that day had quieted him down some, sure, but they'd shaped him as well, and though he never said much at the time, it soon became clear that he'd started seeing things differently somehow, less like a boy and more like a man.

A couple of weeks before his sixteenth birthday, he'd finally announced that he wanted to become a peace officer, and when Walt asked him why, he said it was because he figured justice ought to be dispensed by the law and not by a riled-up lynch-mob, and there was certainly no arguing with that.

So about a year later he left home and got a job with the marshal of Grey Rock, feller name of Jim Cushing. Luke wasn't much more than a glorified errand boy who swept the floors and acted as turnkey whenever the need arose, but to him it was a start, and eighteen months later he became Cushing's junior deputy.

Deputy Marshal of Bakersfield followed, and when old Harry Casey retired, he was elected Town Marshal. These days, Luke was a government man, a Deputy United States Marshal, no less.

But this, Walt suddenly reminded himself, was no time for idle reflection. Somehow the morning had slipped away and the noon stage from Fort Stockton was due in any time now.

It rocked to a dusty halt forty minutes later, and while the reinsman, George French, jumped down from his high seat and gestured that his passengers should head for the common room and a little refreshment, Walt went to work on harness and horseflesh. Almost immediately, however, he spotted Sam making his way back up the slope to the post oak.

Without thinking, he snatched up a fist-size clump of dry earth, shuffled clear of the coach and pitched it at the animal, bawling, *'God damn you, Sam, get away from there!'*

As Sam disappeared into the scrub with his tail between his legs, George and the passengers turned to give Walt a curious look. Frowning, George asked quietly, 'You all right, *amigo?'*

Not trusting himself to speak, Walt only nodded and went back to work, anxious to get the stage the hell out of there as fast as he could.

Thirty minutes later he joined Nellie in the station doorway and watched as George gathered his lines, kicked off the brake, and got his four-horse team headed west again. George only glanced back once, to look at Walt as if he'd never seen him before.

Feeling Nellie's eyes on him too, Walt demanded irritably, 'What is it now?'

'That question again,' she replied, and turned away.

That question again, he thought. *How long can we keep goin' 'til we break?*

Lord, he really didn't know.

He was just about to head for the stable
and fix a hay-and-grain mixture for the
horses when something made him cut
his gaze away to the west.

He didn't see anything at first. Then,
barely visible through the heat-haze, he
made out a rider coming in off the flats
at a weary trot. A lone rider leading a
single pack-horse . . .

A moment later he called Nellie's name,
and when she reappeared in the doorway he snapped, 'Go fetch the Colt, an'
stay out of sight!'

'What — ?'

'Just do it!' he ordered.

Nellie turned her head then, looked
away to the west, and saw the
approaching rider. 'Who . . . ?'

'How do I know?' he spat. 'Jus' get
the Colt!'

Standing her ground instead, she
asked scornfully, 'Again?'

The word slapped him like an open
palm, but he let the accusation in it

pass. 'Again,' he growled. 'Or maybe you didn't see what that feller's fetchin' in with him?'

Nellie took another look, shielding her eyes to see clearer this time. A second later she whispered, 'Oh, Lordy. Is it . . . is it a *body*, Walt?' The rider was close enough now that there could be no doubt. A dead man rolled in a gray woollen blanket was hanging belly-down over the pack-horse, his legs sticking out one side, his bouncing, half-covered head dangling on the other.

Guts tight, Walt turned his attention back to the rider himself, a lean man with broad shoulders and what looked to be long legs, whose dark, wide-brimmed hat threw his face into shadow. As he came nearer, Walt saw that he carried a pistol at his waist and a badge pinned to the chest of his gray placket shirt, a shield into which had been cut a five-pointed star.

'Walt,' said Nellie, her voice suddenly thickening with emotion. 'Walt, it's Luke!'

Walt's face went slack again. *Luke?* *Their* Luke? But almost immediately his relief gave way to an even stronger sense of alarm. They hadn't seen Luke in more than a year. Why did he have to show up again now, of all times?

A few minutes later their boy entered the yard and tied his animals to the remains of an old rear wheel that was leaning against the stable wall. Sam came chasing out of nowhere to greet him, giving Walt a conspicuously wide berth as he did so, and Luke made a playful grab for him before crossing the yard at a jog and gathering Nellie into his arms.

'Ma!' he said warmly. 'As pretty as ever, I see!'

Unable to speak for the moment, Nellie waved the compliment aside and dabbed at her eyes with a small lace handkerchief. While she struggled to compose herself, Luke turned to Walt and offered his right hand, and after the briefest hesitation, Walt took it. 'Son,' he said formally. 'Good to see you again.'

Luke had aged some beyond his four-and-twenty years, and exposure to sun and wind had darkened his skin and lightened his short, sandy hair. Whiskery and travel-marked though he was, however, he was still very much their Luke, with his mother's bright brown eyes and his old man's gaunt features.

'By God,' he said. 'You two are a sight for sore eyes.'

But Walt's attention was fixed on the dead man. 'Brought comp'ny with you, I see.'

Luke grimaced. 'Bank robber name of Tom Guffey,' he replied. 'I caught up with him this morning. I'd have sooner taken him alive, but he didn't give me the choice. I'll stow him out of sight in a minute.'

'I'd appreciate it,' said Nellie, throwing Walt a quick glance. 'Then you'd, ah, better come in out of the sun. Reckon we got some catchin' up to do.'

Luke nodded. 'Reckon we have, at that.'

But fifteen minutes later they were seated at the sawbuck table, sipping fresh-boiled coffee, and trying to think of things to say. Eventually Walt muttered half-heartedly, 'Well, this sure is a turn-up. You, ah, stayin' long, son?'

'Figure I'll head on back to Kelton tomorrow. Doubt that Guffey'll keep much longer'n that.'

'I'd best get to bakin', then,' said Nellie, pushing up from the table. 'I'll fix a special supper tonight an' it'll be like old times.'

But old times had never been like this, filled with furtive looks and invisible barriers, and they all knew it.

As she headed for the kitchen, another uncomfortable silence settled over the common room. To break it, Luke asked how business was and Walt told him it was steady. With the subject thus exhausted, Luke excused himself and went outside with Sam at his heels. In the yard he fished out the makings and rolled himself a smoke.

Walt watched him through one of the station's small, smeared windows, feeling edgier than ever. Eventually, finding it impossible to sit still, he got up, wiped his palms on the seat of his pants, and went to join him.

Luke was squinting up at the post oak.

And Sam had already climbed the slope and was rooting around by the base of the tree.

Seeing that, Walt yelled, '*Sam! Get away from there!*'

The dog flinched at the anger in his voice and took off, vanishing over the far side of the ridge. Recovering himself, Walt made a loose gesture with his right hand and mumbled, 'Damn dog. Always nosin' after somethin'.'

Luke just carried on studying the tree.

'What, ah, what's on your mind, son?' Walt asked with careful indifference.

'Just thinkin',' Luke replied, drawing smoke. ''Bout bein' home again. That old tree an' what we saw happen up there all them years ago.'

'It was a bad business, right enough,' Walt allowed. 'But it turned you into the man you are today, I reckon. Though sometimes I wonder if that was a good thing or a bad one.'

Luke threw him a curious glance. 'How so?'

'Yours is a risky business, son,' said Walt. 'Was you a clerk or a farmer, your ma 'n me, we wouldn't worry so much.'

'I make out okay,' Luke assured him.

They fell silent again until, at length, Luke said, 'Is everything all right, Pa? With you and Ma, I mean?'

'Why shouldn't it be?'

Luke shrugged. 'I get the feelin' you're frettin' over something. An' I don't think it's just over whether or not I'm goin' to stop lead someday.'

'You're imaginin' things, son.'

'I don't think so,' Luke persisted with unnerving certainty. 'You seem awful jumpy, Pa, an' Ma ain't much better. An' what about Sam, there? That dog admires you somethin' fierce as a rule, but today he won't go anywhere near you.' He shook his head. 'There's an atmosphere around here you can cut with a knife, an' I don't like it an' I can't ignore it. If there's anythin' wrong — '

'There isn't.'

'But if there is, I'd want to help.'

Losing patience, Walt heeled around to face him. 'Listen to me, Luke,' he growled. 'If you really want to help, you can start by keepin' your nose out of my — '

'Oh, for God's sake, Walt, tell him!'

Nellie's voice, coming right out of the blue, made both men turn fast. She was standing in the station doorway, close to tears again if the expression on her face was anything to go by.

Staring at Walt, she half-sobbed, 'Tell him an' be done with it!'

'Tell me what?' Luke asked tightly.

His parents continued to look at each other for a long, taut moment. Then Walt let go something that sounded more like a moan than the sigh it was meant to be, and whispered tremulously, 'Oh, Lord, son! What's gonna become of us? We've done killed a man!'

* * *

He swayed then, and his legs would have buckled altogether if Luke hadn't reached out to catch him.

'Ma, you got any whiskey around the place?'

''M all right . . . ' protested Walt.

'The hell you are. Ma?'

'In . . . inside.'

'Get it.'

With Luke supporting him, Walt stumbled back into the dining room and flopped down at the table. Someone — he guessed it was Nellie — shoved a mug into his hands and he smelled strong spirits. He drank, choked, shivered, and then started to feel a mite stronger, and when his vision finally cleared some he saw Luke studying him soberly from the other side of the table, Nellie sitting beside him, weeping softly.

'What's going on here, Pa?' Luke asked gently.

It came in a rush, then, like poison draining from an open wound, and once he started talking, Walt couldn't have stopped the words even if he'd wanted to.

It had happened little under a week earlier. Nellie had been weeding the flower garden when she'd spotted a man coming in from the west, a man afoot, leading a horse that was moving slowly, carefully, not so much tired as injured.

Because you could never be too careful in these parts, she'd immediately fetched Walt, and together they watched the newcomer slowly close the distance between them. The horse, a bay with three white socks, was having a hard time of walking straight. Sand was stuck to his left flank and thigh, indicating that he'd taken a fall, a hard one, judging by the painful way he moved.

Reaching a decision, Walt said, 'Go get the Colt. Chances are we won't need it, but you never can tell. Go fetch it, stay out of sight, an' keep it handy. An' watch that trigger. It's got a light touch.'

Wiping her damp palms on her apron, Nellie turned and vanished inside.

A few minutes later the newcomer limped into the yard, as sore-footed as his mount. He was a thick-set man of an age with Luke, wearing a hickory shirt tucked into riveted jeans, and carrying a gun at his hip. 'Mornin',' he called when he saw Walt.

Walt nodded back. 'You look like you've come a fair piece.'

'That I have,' the man agreed. He had a round, pleasant face, clear blue eyes, and a dusting of light whiskers along his jaw. 'An' the pace has told on poor old Chick, here.'

'What happened?'

Before the newcomer could reply, Sam came over to brush against his legs, and the man bent at the waist to run his free hand along the dog's spine. 'He stepped in a gopher hole, took a fall,' he said after a while. 'Was lucky not to break a leg, I reckon.' Suddenly he thought to introduce himself. 'Name's Johnny Moffat, by the way. Proud to know you.'

Walt shook with him: He had a strong, firm grip. 'Name's Bevan, station manager here. If you'd, ah, care to step inside, the wife'll coffee an' cake you while I take a look at your mount.'

'I'd appreciate that,' said Moffat. 'Thing is, Mr. Bevan — '

And that was when it happened — when the gun in Nellie's hands went off with a roar like thunder, when Nellie herself screamed in a mixture of shock and surprise, when Sam disappeared with a frightened yelp, and when Johnny Moffat's hat was torn from his head and he fell to his knees with his eyes filled with horror, then hit the hardpan face-first.

The area just above and behind his left ear was a red, glistening mess.

Walt watched him go down, his mouth working like that of a fish on a riverbank. His thoughts were scrambled, half-formed. *Wha . . . What did . . . What happened?* And then he heard himself saying it, his voice high, breathless, his tone baffled, confused. He dropped to his own knees, went to touch the dead man and drew back when he heard Nellie let go another long, awful wail.

He looked up, saw her standing in the station doorway, the Colt looking as big as a saddle-gun in her tiny, work-roughened hands, smoke still drifting lazily from the long barrel like the ghost of a snake making its getaway.

Pale as chalk, Nellie muttered, 'Walt, it . . . the gun, it . . . it jus' went off . . .'

He stared at her for a long, dumb moment. Of course it went off. That damn' smoke-belcher always had been unreliable, that's why he'd warned her about the hair trigger. But then he remembered Nellie wiping her palms on her apron. Maybe those damp, slippery fingers had made what happened even more inevitable.

'Is he . . . ?' she began.

Bracing himself, Walt checked the body. There was no heartbeat that he could detect.

'He's dead,' he said in someone else's voice.

'Oh God,' said Nellie. 'I killed him, Walt. I killed him!'

★   ★   ★

'And then you buried him,' guessed Luke. 'Up there, 'neath the oak.'

She eyed him bleakly. 'We're not proud of it, son,' she husked.

'Then why the heck didn't you just lay the poor sonofabuck out someplace cool and report what happened to the authorities?' he demanded.

Walt sat forward. 'Because there was always the chance they might not've believed us!' he rasped. 'An' even if they had, what would it have told them about us, Luke? That we're gettin' old, that's what. Too damn old to think straight an' too damn addled to act right.' He snorted. 'You think the stage line'd keep us on out here after that? Oh, no. Even if they gave us the benefit of the doubt, we'd still end up losin' everythin', boy, everythin'. This place. Our jobs. Our pension.' He shook his head. 'An' if it went the other way, if they decided we'd killed that feller deliberate . . . ' His voice cracked. 'Your ma'n me, how long you suppose we'd last in prison? How long you suppose we'd last without *each other*?'

Luke sighed, recognizing the truth of his words. 'So you decided to bury the body and just keep quiet about it.'

'I dragged him up there, to the tree,' Walt confessed miserably. 'Damn near killed me to do it. Then I dug a grave, a shallow one. I didn't have the strength to dig it deep, the ground was too hard. I rolled him in, covered him up, figured to go back, make a better job of it next day, but . . . I couldn't go up there again, son, I jus' couldn't.'

Walt's eyes suddenly went large and desperate. 'Aw, son,' he said, 'you can't know what it's been like, living with it. We've hardly slept, we've hardly spoke. It's been . . . '

He broke off then and, unable to fight it any longer, he started sobbing.

Luke stood up and strode outside. After a moment Walt and Nellie went after him. He got a shovel from one of the storage sheds, the same shovel Walt had used five days earlier, then climbed the slope with Sam forging out ahead of him.

When he reached the base of the tree, he examined the ground for a while, then shook his head, slammed the shovel into the ground and came back down to rejoin them.

Walt, a smaller, deflated image of his former self, said quietly, 'What are you gonna do, son? Turn us in?'

Luke said, 'I ought to. But there's no one up there, Pa.'

'What?'

'That grave you dug — it's empty.'

*   *   *

Luke studied them both for a thoughtful moment then said, 'I think you better come with me.'

Still in shock, they followed him meekly back across the yard to the shed. The late Tom Guffey, still rolled in the blanket, was stretched out against the right-side wall, exactly where Luke had dumped him earlier. Now he knelt beside the dead man, threw back the blanket and said, 'Look familiar?'

Nellie grabbed Walt's arm and Walt grabbed the doorframe. 'That's him!' he breathed. 'Johnny Moffat.'

'It's Tom Guffey,' corrected Luke.

Nellie shook her head. 'I don't . . . '

'This sonofabuck tried to rob the bank at Kelton about a week ago,' said Luke. 'But he didn't reckon on the manager telling him to go to hell. He went crazy, shot the manager dead, crippled the marshal, an' then lit out empty-handed, knocking down and killing a seven- year-old boy on his way out of town.'

'Are you sure it's the same man?' asked Walt.

'Oh, it's Guffey, right enough,' Luke replied. 'Anyway, this is how I read it — Guffey lit out of Kelton and rode like the devil 'til his horse took a fall. Then he came here looking to buy or steal a replacement. But before he could do any such thing, Ma killed him. Or *thought* she did.'

'I shot him in the head!' said Nellie.

An old neckerchief was knotted around the dead man's head. Luke slipped it off so that they could see the blood-encrusted gouge that scored Guffey's skull just above and behind the left ear. 'You shot him, right enough, but you didn't kill him. You knocked him cold and when Pa couldn't find his heartbeat you naturally assumed you'd killed him.'

'But I buried him!' Walt protested.

'In a shallow grave you didn't even fill in properly,' Luke countered. 'He likely regained consciousness later, feeling sick as hell and with his brain half-scrambled. He got out of that grave, staggered away and decided to hole up someplace 'til he was healed. That'd fit the facts.'

'Why?'

'Because when I happened across him, he'd fixed himself a rough-and-ready camp down along Quitman Creek, and he was afoot, no sign of a horse anywhere. I rode in on him by accident, didn't even know he was there 'til he jumped up and started shooting at me. I fired back, got him with the first shot.'

'Which means . . . ' murmured Walt, with a kind of wonder.

'Which means you didn't kill 'Johnny Moffat',' said Luke. 'I did. You folks didn't kill anyone.'

Walt rested his chin on his chest for a moment. The heady rush of relief and gratitude was almost too much to handle. He felt Nellie's hand on his arm and covered it with one of his own. 'It's all right, now,' he whispered. 'Everythin's all right.'

She nodded.

Allowing the blanket to drop back over the dead man's face, Luke straightened up. 'Well,' he sighed, 'you folks got an ugly hole up on yonder rim needs filling in. Reckon I'll go up there and see to it.'

Walt drew a deep breath, squared his shoulders, and cleared his throat. Reaching down to scrub Sam's head affectionately, he sniffed noisily and said with some of his old humor, 'Come on, you mangy critter. Let's go watch Luke do some work!'

THE END

We do hope that you have enjoyed reading this large print book.

Did you know that all of our titles are available for purchase?

We publish a wide range of high quality large print books including:
**Romances, Mysteries, Classics
General Fiction
Non Fiction and Westerns**

Special interest titles available in large print are:
**The Little Oxford Dictionary
Music Book, Song Book
Hymn Book, Service Book**

Also available from us courtesy of Oxford University Press:
**Young Readers' Dictionary
(large print edition)
Young Readers' Thesaurus
(large print edition)**

For further information or a free brochure, please contact us at:
**Ulverscroft Large Print Books Ltd.,
The Green, Bradgate Road, Anstey,
Leicester, LE7 7FU, England.
Tel:** (00 44) 0116 236 4325
Fax: (00 44) 0116 234 0205

Other titles in the
Linford Western Library:

SHOOTOUT AT CLEARWATER SPRINGS

Aaron Adams

River Bow Ranch is in big trouble: owing money to the bank, and with only a small, sickly herd. It looks as if Mark Merkel will be forced to hand over his business to his ruthless neighbour, Connor MacPherson, who has been eyeing the River Bow for some time. But Mark's son David refuses to be defeated, and has an audacious plan to save the ranch. Faced with an implacable enemy, and with a murderer in their midst, can the Merkels succeed?

SKELETON HAND

C. J. Sommers

Three cowboys, cut loose from the Domino ranch, head south to seek work elsewhere. Caught in a storm, they take shelter in an abandoned trapper's cabin, where they make two startling discoveries — a hoard of gold squirreled away, and a skeleton holding a hand of cards. Taking the cash, they journey on — but find themselves drawn into a lethal game with a band of killers. It seems the skeleton isn't holding the only deadly hand . . .

JOURNEY INTO JEOPARDY

Mark Bannerman

Former Pinkerton detective Frank Glengarry is called out of retirement to take on one final task: the delivery of a ransom to the kidnappers of Lucille Glassner, daughter of a US senator. Though assured there will be no danger, Glengarry is travelling to one of the remotest corners of California — and is about to fall foul of the law. Forced onto a trail littered with lynchings, greed, vengeance, murder and double-dealing, his only means of escape is to face up to those who want him dead . . .

SHOTGUN CHARADE

Ethan Flagg

Cowboy Laramie Juke helps out a new buddy whose family is being harassed by Highspade Jack Daley, the unscrupulous Mayor of Jacinto. Attempting to get rid of the Cavendish clan, who have discovered a rich gold seam — the source of which hides beneath his own land — Daley has hired the notorious Shotgun Murphy. But when Juke arrives in Jacinto, he is mistaken for the gunman . . . leading to a deadly encounter where nothing is as it seems, and no one can be trusted.

A MAN CALLED DRIFTER

Steve Hayes

Ingrid Bjorkman had been kidnapped. But was she just the bait in a trap meant to snare her would-be rescuers? In their long, gunsmoke-filled lives, three men — Gabriel Moonlight, Latigo Rawlins, and the man known only as Drifter — had made more than their fair share of enemies. And when the trio took to the trail, they had two more shooters to back their play: Raven, daughter of Ingrid — and Deputy US Marshal Liberty Mercer, daughter of Drifter . . .

THE DEVIL'S MARSHAL

I. J. Parnham

When Lucinda Latimer is accused of murdering Archibald Harper, her bounty hunter brother Brodie is convinced of her innocence. Vowing to find the culprit, he turns up a witness in the form of drunken varmint Wilfred Clay — who, minutes after admitting to seeing the real killer, is shot to death on his own front porch. All the clues point to the murderer being Derrick Shelby — the man known as 'the devil's marshal'. The only trouble is, Derrick died a year ago . . .